The
DISAPPEARING
TEACHER

The
DISAPPEARING
TEACHER

Conrad Nowels

SCHOLASTIC BOOK SERVICES
New York Toronto London Auckland Sydney Tokyo

ISBN 0-590-31464-5

Published by Scholastic Book Services, a division of Scholastic Magazines, Inc.

12 11 10 9 8 7 6 5 4 3 2 1   2   1 2 3 4 5 6/8

Printed in the U. S. A.   06

1.

If you've ever read any books or stories that were about teenage girls, you know that there are certain things that most of them have in common. First, the girl they're about is usually somebody whom everybody can identify with. Not too pretty, not ugly or too fat or too thin or too built, and while she's never exactly an airhead she's never any genius either.

In short, she's pretty much your basic American Schoolgirl, surrounded by your basic American Schoolgirl cast of supporting characters; like her special crew of buddies who sip Cokes and munch burgers, pizza, and tacos with her. Or the hopeless out-of-it parents who cause her mucho grief when they don't understand her, but who inevitably turn out to have hearts of gold and rally to her side when the final crisis occurs.

Of course that's usually inspired by another member of the cast, the guy her heart throbs for but who doesn't even know she's alive. At least not in the beginning. This is generally due to his

1

being dazzled at the time by the local high school witch, your basic beautiful but superficial siren who has him under her heartless spell while poor Ms. Everybody-Can-Identify-With pines nobly for true love.

Until the end, when the boy in question miraculously sees the light at last and bestows his affections on our heroine. The rotten seductress gets her come-uppance and everybody lives happily ever after. Just like life, right?

Wrong. If you've learned as much about life as I have in my sixteen years you know it isn't all cut and dried, black or white, good or bad. Which is where I come in. I'm the rotten one. I'm the witch you've read about in all those goony stories. At least that's what people seem to think. Just because the boyfriends of the Wendy Wimps of the world find me more interesting. Just because I sometimes can't resist taking an occasional harmless, humorous dig at little Ms. Tess Trueheart, they call me a cat. It's because of that that all this wild stuff I'm going to tell you about happened to me last year.

To begin with, I was in Hollywood. Like everything else in my life that sounds a lot better than it really was. Just the word "Hollywood" opens up visions of glamor, of pool parties, of movie and TV stars, California Soul and Surf, the place where it's HAPPENING.

Except that what was happening for me was punishment. That's right, I was sent out to Hollywood for punishment, for being a bad girl. At least that's what my mother had in mind.

"I am fed up, Lisa, with your wild behavior.

I have had it with you, young lady. And you'd better wipe that smirk off your face if you know what's good for you. Do you hear me? This is the last time you are ever going to get away with flaunting your — "

But why bore you with that particular LP, some version of which I'm sure you've heard too, if you have a mother.

What had set her off was that little twit, Emily Kemp. Or, to be more exact, Emily Kemp's mother. It seems that Mrs. Kemp made it her business to repeat Emily's lies to my mother the night of the Ladies Ecology League Masquerade Ball. She actually had the grotesque nerve to insinuate that I'd stolen Emily's boyfriend away from her by letting him take (in her phrase) "liberties" with me.

Emily Kemp, of course, rots. But even if she didn't, I wouldn't let that nerd Richard Price even hold my hand. You'll understand the entire scene when I tell you that Mrs. Kemp just happens to be the Chairperson of the Ladies Ecology League. Just like she was for the Junior League and still is for just about every one of the socially important things in town. Incidentally, that town (my hometown, though you'd never guess from the way I'm treated) is Saratoga Springs, New York, and a big part of the punishment for me was being sent away just as the summer racing meet was to start. Not that I'm into racing that much but the only thing that makes life worth living in a dead end like Saratoga Springs is when the thoroughbreds come there for one glorious month every summer. Which of course

was the whole idea behind sending me away —
I would miss all the parties and dances and
picnics on the racepark grounds and all the other
great things that all of us kids look forward to
all through the long, dreary winter.

So, for the sake of my mother's social aspira-
tions, there I was, convicted and sentenced without a trial. I was going to tell her what really
happened, how Richard Price practically slobbers
and drools every time he comes near a girl (in a
way you can't blame the poor guy — he's been
stuck with Emily Kemp ever since the eighth
grade). But then I thought to myself, "If that's
how little she thinks of her own flesh and blood,
then she doesn't deserve any explanation." So I
just told her that she knew me and she knew
the Kemps and she could make up her own mind
as to what the truth really was. And, of course,
the next thing I knew I was on a plane for Los
Angeles.

You're probably thinking to yourself, "Oh,
yeah, punish me, send me to Hollywood, please!"
But that's because you don't know my aunt,
Catharine Farraday. Come to think of it, I didn't
really know her either. Which was the excuse
my mother used on my father for shipping me
out of town (not daring to repeat the vulgar
scandal to him, of course) like the village leper.

"After all, Craig," I heard her softening him
up while she was mixing their before-dinner
cocktail, "Aunt Kay is nearly seventy, and this
may be the last opportunity Lisa will ever have
to get to know her."

"But why is it suddenly so important for her

to get to know Aunt Kay this summer?" My father's puzzled voice floated up to where I happened to be accidentally perched at the top of the stairs.

"Darling, you know how crucial role models are for a girl in her formative years. Women's consciousness is rising and an achiever like Aunt Kay, a successful attorney, would be very good for Lisa."

"Well, there's no doubt it would be an experience," my father chuckled drily. "But the whole summer . . . with an old woman . . . ?"

"There's the question of discipline as well," my mother went on, moving in for the kill. "Aunt Kay is a very disciplined person. She has always had the drive to accomplish things in the world. It would be a healthy contrast for Lisa. You know I have always been too soft and yielding . . . just a little old-fashioned homemaker. . . ."

"I kind of like little old-fashioned home-makers . . . ," my father murmured just before that familiar pause in their conversation which meant that they were kissing. Give them their due. They really love each other and aren't ashamed to show it.

To get back to my case. Did you catch that bit about discipline? That, naturally, was the point of the whole thing. Aunt Catharine (actually, she's my great-aunt, having been married to my father's uncle, Jack Farraday) is a Farraday family legend, a cross between a fire-breathing dragon and Einstein. My father, in fact, has a favorite retort whenever one of Aunt Kay's caustic diatribes is relayed to him via the family grapevine. "The old lady simply does not suffer fools gladly, that's all."

So there it was. My mother was throwing me to the lions. From all I'd heard I have to admit my Great Aunt Catharine sounded pretty scary. Anyway, that was certainly what my mother was counting on, which was probably the only thing that helped me keep a partly open mind. Oh, I almost forgot, Aunt Kay was also the only woman in the family who had never had any children. I suspect my mother believed that in some mysterious fashion, I would bring a ray of youthful sunshine into Aunt Kay's drab existence, especially since a few years ago Aunt Kay had lost her sight. Which all tied in with my mother's master plan — the rehabilitation of her incorrigible, willful daughter through the responsibility of taking care of a dried-up, despairing, decrepit old lady.

Which, as you are about to find out, should probably go down with Hitler's invasion of Russia and Nixon's law and order administration as examples of things that didn't exactly turn out the way they were supposed to.

2.

If the doorbell or phone should happen to ring during dinner in the old, dark wood dining room of my Great Aunt Kay's suite at the Chateau Marmont, ordinarily it is Mrs. DiPasquale who answers it. But that evening, my fifth in Los Angeles (I had been marking them off on my bedroom wall like old-time prisoners used to do on the stones of their dungeons), when the door buzzed I made sure to get to it first. Which wasn't very difficult because Mrs. DiPasquale, who, despite a name which makes her sound like she should be middle-aged and stout, is young and attractive and a former go-go dancer, was in the kitchen putting the finishing touches on the main course.

There were two reasons for making sure to get the door. The first was that Mrs. DiPasquale has strict orders from my aunt not to admit anyone who isn't either personally known to her or doesn't have an appointment. Well, since I had only met the person buzzing that afternoon he couldn't qualify as the first and he certainly didn't have an appointment. In fact I didn't see how anybody got appointments anymore, the way that Aunt Kay had practically turned into a hermit. It wasn't so much that she'd lost any of the spirit and grit I'd always heard about, it was just that she didn't seem interested in doing anything anymore. For instance, she absolutely refused to get a Seeing Eye dog or to go to the Lighthouse for the Blind or any of the other organizations that are around to help handicapped people.

"My darling Lisa," she informed me when I brought it up as tactfully as possible, "the afflictions which accrue to us in life, like the honors that we earn, are only demeaned and cheapened by trying to institutionalize them. Life is the one great personal gamble left in a civilization which seems determined to de-personalize us and it is futile to try to lay off the action."

At first I didn't understand at all, but then I thought that probably it had to do with living as long as Aunt Kay had. She'd come to feel that, good or bad, everything in her life was *hers*. And that's what really turned her on and kept her alive. That she was doing the one thing nobody else could, living her own, personal, exclusive life. Whether you understand that or not (and I don't know many kids, including myself, who feel that way about their lives) you'd have to admit that my Aunt Kay could be pretty outrageous and understand why I wanted to get to the door first and prepare this poor guy for what he was walking into. Actually I should've prepared myself . . . for seeing him with clothes on.

In case that calls for an explanation, it was simply that I had spent most of the daylight hours since I arrived tanning myself alongside the Chateau Marmont swimming pool. I'll confess that it wasn't only because I wanted to get rid of the yucchhy white pallor my skin had. The fact that the lifeguard was about as cute a guy as I had ever seen might have had a little to do with it too. Except that all week long I could just as well have been back in Saratoga for all the attention he paid to me. Not that I'm one of those conceited girls who thinks all a boy has to do is take one look at her for him to get stars in his eyes, but I have been known to attract at least *some* attention in my bikini. Finally it got so frustrating that I carried the sandwiches Mrs. DiPasquale had made for my lunch over to where he was sitting and just staring out into space.

"Hey, man, lighten up," I said in my palsiest tone. "You look as though you're carrying the whole world's problems on your back."

Then, since he didn't respond, I sat down alongside him and offered one of Mrs. Di's sandwiches made with Italian ham that her grandfather cures in his own smokehouse.

"I'm not hungry, thanks," he mumbled, not even looking at me. Which was followed by a long silence while I fought back the urge to flee.

"My name is Lisa," I said brightly, sticking out my hand. Still very palsy. After a moment he sort of clasped my hand and said, "Ron." He still didn't look at me.

"How long do you have for a lunch break?" I

9

asked as soon as he'd let my hand drop like it was a bubbling hot slice of pizza.

"Half-hour. Why?"

"That won't be long enough." I took a deep breath. "You'd better come over tonight then. About eight o'clock. Suit 525. It'll be better there, anyway, because you can tell my aunt too. She's good at helping people with their problems."

"Hey!" He was finally looking at me. I could tell because I could see his teeth through his wide-open mouth. They were as perfect as the rest of him.

"What're you talking about?"

"I'm not sure, exactly," I responded blandly while I wrapped the remains of Mrs. Di's incredible sandwiches. "But usually with guys your age and general appearance I would say it's woman trouble. But whatever it is that's been wrecking your head you'll find that you'll feel better when you talk about it. And, like I said, my aunt has a way of helping people in trouble."

"What is she, a detective or something?"

It was funny the way he said it. You had to hear it. He wasn't sneering, it was more like he was grasping at a straw.

"No," I said, "but she does employ them. Private detectives, I mean." Actually that wasn't a complete lie. I'd heard about a case my aunt had where after much soul-searching about the morality and ethics of doing it, she had used a private detective. Of course that had been before I was born and Aunt Kay wasn't exactly active in her law practice anymore but you can't blurt out every intimate detail of your relative's business to a perfect stranger.

"Well," I said, getting up, "you'd better tell me your last name so I can introduce you tonight. Mine's Farraday, same as my aunt."

"Wait." I felt his hand on my arm. "It's Van Cleave. Ron Van Cleave. How did you know? About something bothering me, I mean?"

"I can't imagine. Unless it had something to do with the way you've been staring into space day after day. Everybody here could've drowned for all the attention you've been paying."

"Oh, most of them here are just down for the sunbathing, anyway." He shrugged and tossed his head in the direction of two girls who'd obviously decided to increase the extent of their tans and the scenery at the same time by wearing the tiniest bikinis. "I guess you've been kind of watching me, haven't you?"

I turned and met his eyes straight on. They were hazel and probably would have been very nice if they hadn't been so full of worry.

"See you at eight," I reminded him, not wanting to let that moment get out of hand.

"I've still got that half-hour of lunch break," he said, not letting go of my arm.

"Well, if you really want to."

"I don't know if you're just some variety of Southern California Crazy or what." He tried to smile and I could see that under other circumstances I might like it very much if he did. "But *I* will be one if I don't tell somebody about this thing."

And he did.

And then there he was at eight sharp standing in my aunt's doorway looking even cuter, all spruced up in a sports shirt and jacket. My head was spinning and only partly because I had to figure out some way of conning Aunt Kay into keeping the appointment I had made for her without her permission. And I just had to, because of what Ron had told me that afternoon sitting alongside the pool.

"It's all right, Mrs. DiPasquale," I called out, seeing her coming through the hall from the kitchen, wiping her hands on her apron. "Ron — Mr. Van Cleave — has an appointment."

"Really? With whom?"

"I don't know how Aunt Kay does that — glides silently into rooms when she can't see and all — but I turned to find her standing behind me, her blue-tinted glasses opaque in the dim light of the foyer. I couldn't tell if she was as angry as the tone of her voice.

"Uh . . . Mrs. Farraday, I'm Ron Van Cleave. Uh . . . I really appreciate Lisa, I mean . . . your confidential assistant . . . making an appointment for me to see you. I mean, with your being so busy with that case you're trying before the Supreme Court and all."

Poor Ron was shifting awkwardly from one foot to the other in the doorway. Which was exactly what I was doing mentally. Telling him that my aunt was trying a case before the Supreme Court and that I was her confidential assistant, which had popped out so naturally that afternoon at the pool, no longer seemed like such a brainstorm.

"Lisa, the soup is getting cold. Please explain to this young man that I see people only — "

"Only when it's a really interesting and unusual case. And his sure is." I felt a little bolder because Aunt Kay had just slipped in a little fib of her own, the kind she was prone to when her privacy was threatened. The soup was already cold because it was vichyssoise, a cold potato and leek soup (the potatoes unpeeled for the sake of nutrition, of all yucchhy things). "When you hear his story, Aunt Kay, I'm sure you'll agree."

"I'm sure I would, dear, but as my 'confidential assistant' you must know how tied up I am with my . . . uh . . . case before the Supreme Court?"

Even having been there for only five days I had become familiar with that particular tone of my aunt's voice. It was time to play my trump card.

"I'm awfully sorry, Mr. Van Cleave," I told him in my most gracious tone, "but I'm afraid that I have over-stepped my authority. Just because your father is a member of the Chevaliers de Bourgogne was no reason for me to invite you to dinner on the spur of the moment like this. Please accept my apol — "

"Your father is one of the Chevaliers de Bourgogne?" Aunt Kay's tone had undergone a subtle change. That "Chevaliers de Bourgogne" (they're apparently the most prestigious gourmet society in America) bit was something I'd picked up out of a copy of *Gourmet* magazine I'd seen on her desk. My aunt's obsession with gourmet cooking was a family legend. And joke. After my great-uncle died, she'd really gotten into health

13

foods too, and tried to blend them into her gourmet recipes.

Ron caught my pleading look. "Well . . . yes . . . my father is really involved in . . . that," he gulped, manfully backing me up. I could have kissed him for picking up on it so quickly.

"You will have to make allowances, Mr. Van Cleave," purred Aunt Kay, her attitude completely changed as she motioned him inside and led the way back toward the dining room. "It will be a case of accepting pot luck."

You'd never know my aunt can't see the way she maneuvers through the rooms of that sprawling old apartment. She loved the Chateau Marmont, she said, because the apartments, with their high ceilings and big old rooms, reminded her of the west side of Manhattan where she grew up. My Uncle Jack, who was my grandfather's oldest brother, had been a movie producer, and after he died, my aunt sold their big home on Lloydcrest Drive in Beverly Hills and moved into the old hotel on Sunset Boulevard.

Through the cold soup and the liver loaf garnished with soybean curd, clear through to the goat cheeses and fresh papaya, Ron told his story while Aunt Kay listened. She was a great listener once you got her to put her mind to it. She'd interrupted only twice. The first was to remind me that she hadn't forgotten how I'd gotten her into it.

"Lisa, dear," she asked, her voice dripping honey, "haven't you forgotten your pad and pen? As my 'confidential assistant' you know it is your responsibility to take down everything that's said."

The second time was just to ask Ron's opinion as to how the food compared with what his father and the Chevaliers de Bourgogne served. He lied, but not very convincingly, which wasn't surprising considering that he hadn't been able to make it as an actor which was what had brought him to L.A. from New York City. The only trouble was that he needed tutoring if he was going to be able to major in business finance and economics, the area that most interested him. Some kids he'd gotten friendly with had recommended somebody who, they told him, had gotten ever single kid she'd ever tutored into college, even though she herself had only taught high school and was soon to retire. To help cover the extra expense, Ron worked out an arrangement to do the heavy work around his tutor's house, as part of his pay, which is where his story really began.

3.

Ron's tutor was a lady and a legend. Her name was Emmáline Williams and what made her a legend was the incredible amount of time and trouble she took with her students, whether they were the regular ones from the high school or the more advanced ones she tutored in the summer for college courses.

"I don't care what the kids say about her" — Ron was nibbling politely on a slice of papaya — "Miss Williams was an incredible person."

"What did they say?" Aunt Kay's query was equally polite.

"Oh, you know how some kids are, one semester of psychology and they think they're Sigmund Freud. They were put off by how intense she was about helping them, said she was just 'over-compensating' because she had never married. They said she was 'forming unnatural attachments' because she'd never had any kids herself."

Then, realizing that might not have been the

most tactful of subjects to get into with my aunt, Ron quickly went back to the point.

"Then, suddenly, a little while ago she changed. Overnight she became a different person. She had *no* time for anybody, didn't want to come to the door even when she knew she had students coming. And the phone? One time I was coming to do the chores and I could hear the phone ringing from outside, ringing right off the hook. I thought maybe she was out, and since she'd given me a key I ran in to answer it, but she was there all the time. Just standing there staring at the phone while it rang."

He shook his head. "It was really weird. It was like just seeing or hearing the kids got her all uptight."

Aunt Kay offered him some coffee and while I poured it for him I noticed how taut the muscles were in his face. He was really under a lot of tension.

"I thought Miss Williams and I had gotten real close," he went on after stirring some cream into his cup. "She seemed to take a special liking to me for some reason. It was funny but somehow it seemed like it was because I'd given up the idea of being an actor for economics and finance which was what she loved. She seemed to feel that way even more," he laughed self-consciously, "than my father!"

I should mention here that Ron had told me earlier that his father, whom he'd lived with practically alone in this big old house somewhere on the New Jersey shore after his mother had run away when he was twelve, was a very successful advertising executive.

Aunt Kay merely nodded. If the truth were told, her opinion of advertising executives was even lower than of actors.

"Sometimes, after I'd finished out in the garden or come back from doing her shopping for her, Miss Williams would ask me if I'd like some coffee or tea or milk and we'd sit around and talk. Really get into things. She used to like me to tell her my reasons for giving up acting and getting into finance. She would listen intently and nod and say, 'It's only proper in the evolution of a young person; now you have gone past the phase of showing off your exterior self in favor of the next stage of development. Which is to utilize your *interior* self, the real stuff you've got inside you.'"

"All that was before she started changing, wasn't it?" I prodded him back on the track.

"Mmmmmm." Ron nodded and put down his coffee cup. "It all seemed to come to a climax right after that phone call I told you about where she wouldn't answer. The last thing I used to do in the evening was take out the bag of garbage from the kitchen. Only that night I remembered I had left my sunglasses on the sink, and when I went back for them I heard Miss Williams in the dining room. She was huddled over the table and she seemed to have a picture in her hand, not a photograph, more like a picture that was torn out of a newspaper or something. She was shaking her head and moaning over and over in this pathetic voice: "Nairobi . . .

Nairobi . . . Nairobi. . . ." She must've sensed my presence because she jumped up, covering the picture, and stalked out of the room saying something about how she couldn't have a stranger prowling about and she'd have to have my key back."

"Let me understand this, Mr. Van Cleave." Aunt Kay's tone was a little doubtful. "You found Miss Williams holding some sort of picture torn from a publication and murmuring the name of the capital city of Kenya?"

"Well, that's what I thought she was saying at the time but I'm pretty positive the picture was of a girl."

"You said it was at night. Were the lights on in the dining room?"

"No."

"And looking over her shoulder you could be positive?" Aunt Kay's tone was coldly precise. I could see what she must have been like cross-examining people on the witness stand.

"I didn't say I was *absolutely* positive." Ron seemed to be having second thoughts.

"I'll bet it was a girl," I put in loyally. Ron didn't even bother to glance my way. He was intent on getting his point across.

"Whatever it was a picture of, Miss Williams didn't want me to see it, that I *am* positive of. And I'm sure she was crying, besides."

I leaned over to pour him another cup of coffee but he motioned me not to, explaining that he'd had enough trouble sleeping these nights.

"Of course, I felt about this big," he went on

to my aunt, holding his thumb and forefinger about an inch apart. "I was really embarrassed, you know, so when I saw this crumpled ball of paper on the dining room table I automatically picked it up to put it with the rest of the garbage, without thinking."

He hesitated. "Anyway, that was the last time I saw Miss Williams. When I came for my lesson the next afternoon I found the place locked, and when I used my key to get in finally, the house was deserted. All her personal things, clothes, books, stuff like that were gone. I felt funny looking around without her being there so I only stayed a minute. Her car was gone, too."

"How about luggage?" I interrupted.

"I don't know. I'd never noticed any before so I wouldn't know if any was missing. The next day I went back again after trying by phone for a few hours but it was an instant replay. After that I called the board of education but all I got there was a statement that 'Miss Emmaline Williams had terminated her relationship with this institution.' That was all they cared about, and since I'd heard Miss Williams say many times that she was 'the last of the Williamses' I didn't know where to turn next. It seemed I was up against a blank wall."

"Blank, perhaps, Mr. Van Cleave, but not necessarily insidious, which is what you, I fear, are about to suggest." Aunt Kay's voice was calm, even (which was *definitely* insidious) slightly bored. "Surely many innocent alternatives suggest themselves: a call from a friend, some business or professional emergency, a well-deserved vacation from her task of opening and shaping young minds?"

"Miss Williams didn't have any friends." Ron sounded very stubborn. "Her only business was her students, and she never took a vacation because, she said, 'it would be an admission there was something I would rather be doing than teaching and then what would ever be the point of coming back to put all my energy into something that wasn't the most important thing in the world for me?' "

I saw a faint smile play across Aunt Kay's lips and I thought that, without ever having met her, she was growing fond of Ron's Miss Emmaline Williams.

"Besides, there's another reason why I don't think Miss Williams' disappearing like that was . . . uh . . . innocent." Ron seemed embarrassed. "You'll probably think I'm conceited but . . . well . . . I know she looked forward to my tutoring sessions. And that one, the one she wasn't there for the day she disappeared, that was to be the second part of her favorite lecture, 'The Evaluation of Corporate Securities.' We'd done the first part the week before and I could tell how it pleased her when I started picking up on what she was laying down. To be able to get her ideas and theories across to somebody, wow, that was really close to her heart. It would have to be something really heavy to make her miss that."

There was a silence while Aunt Kay digested Ron's last piece of information. Then she pushed back her chair and got up.

"Why don't we continue in the study?" she said.

She didn't wait for an answer so Ron and I trooped dutifully along behind her as Mrs. Di began to clear the table.

4.

The study is my aunt's favorite space. It has a beautiful Oriental rug, a magnificent globe of the world alongside her desk, with the important places marked in braille, pen and ink sketches of various movie actors made by my Great Uncle Jack on the sets of his pictures, and several really comfortable chairs.

Ron had picked up his story again. "Well, not knowing what else to do, my next concern was finding another tutor and even before that, another job. Which was how I ended up here at the pool and met — "

He turned and looked at me for almost the first time since he began.

"Yes, I have ascertained that part of it." Aunt Kay's tone was still very businesslike. "But I have yet to ascertain what you expect from me."

"Well . . ." Ron was taken aback. "I thought that was obvious . . ."

"To find her!" I couldn't help blurting it out.

"I'm an attorney, Mr. Van Cleave." Aunt Kay

was very composed. "That is more properly a job for the police."

Ron nodded. "Well, I actually did try them, but they were no help. They sent me to the Missing Persons Bureau. But they had the same attitude as you . . . about her going on vacation or something. And since no relative had come forward to make an official request . . . Well, they were very polite and took my number and address and said they'd be sure to let me know if there were further developments. But I could tell they were mostly amused at what they considered my overactive imagination. I could see them shoot little looks at each other when I started to tell them about how she had changed so suddenly."

"Their attitude is not surprising. Speaking of your imagination, what exactly do you imagine happened? You do have a theory, don't you?"

Ron leaned forward, putting his fists on the desk. "Well, not exactly, but I have been wracking my brain, trying to come up with some sort of clue that makes sense. But . . ."

"Actually you are thinking she might have met with what is referred to in mystery stories as 'foul play,' aren't you? Only you don't want to face that." Aunt Kay's voice was crisp, almost cold. Again, I had a picture of her cross-examining someone.

"I didn't say that." Ron's voice lacked conviction.

"Please, Mr. Van Cleave. I am not obtuse. Throughout your narrative almost every time you have had occasion to refer to your tutor you

24

have chosen the past tense as though you felt she no longer existed."

Ron didn't seem to have any answer to that so Aunt Kay continued. "My niece was right about one thing. This does present an interesting problem. But hardly one to be solved by an old woman who had a most ordinary law practice. Notwithstanding, of course," she cleared her throat, "my sudden dramatic appearance before the Supreme Court. I am afraid I really don't see how I can be of any — "

"Aunt Kay!" I just knew it was up to me. The whole thing would slip away unless I did something. "What about that case my parents were always talking about? Where you found that missing oil company executive who'd disappeared?"

"My role in that has always received the benefit of fanciful embroidery from your family. Actually it was the usual missing husband situation and his discovery was the result of a good deal of luck combined with painstaking effort by a private detective with the unlikely name of Conrad Moog. Dear old Mr. Moog." I could have sworn she sighed. "He passed away some years ago, I believe. . . ."

"Mrs. Farraday." Ron's urgent tone brought her back to the present.

"Mrs. Farraday, I've been saving up to buy a Suzuki 1000 . . . a motorcycle. By next week I should have about fifteen hundred dollars. I'm sorry it isn't more and I don't know how far that would go, but if you would take it for now I would be trying to get more . . . if you would do what you could." He shook his head. "Nobody seems to care. I don't know where else to turn."

"You realize that you would be spending all your money on what may very well turn out to be a wild goose chase?" Aunt Kay cleared her throat. "That most probably your Miss Williams has just gone off somewhere in defiance of your estimation of her temperament but in complete accord with the vagaries of the human spirit? In which eventuality she will not be grateful for your efforts to intrude into her privacy?"

Ron shook his head as if he were trying to clear it. "I don't care about anybody being grateful. I just feel people ought to care about one another."

"A sentiment almost everyone would subscribe to but almost none would pay for. Young master Van Cleave, you have inadvertently touched the one weak link in my armor of indifference to my fellow man. Unfortunately, I too, am an incurable romantic. It is a rare occasion that I find such another."

"Does that mean you'll do it?"

"It means that I, I mean, *we*, my confidential assistant and I, will try. Now. What about that clue of yours?

"That crumpled ball of paper you mentioned, was there anything written on it?"

Ron was staring at her. "You must be reading my mind," he said finally, pulling the wrinkled sheet of paper from his pocket and extending it across the desk.

There was a moment in which nothing happened.

"Oh! You can't . . ." Ron was stuttering awkwardly. "I . . . didn't . . . I'm sorry."

"Don't be." Aunt Kay's tone was sharp. She can't abide pity about her sight. I'd never thought to mention it and I forget Aunt Kay is so adept that people can be fooled at first. She was going on.

"I would rather think of it as an act of God for which nature has compensated by sharpening the remainder of my perceptions. Or so you had better hope since you are hiring them."

I reached over and took the paper from Ron. The only thing on it was the word "Niobe" scrawled over it several times in shaky handwriting. I told Aunt Kay and she asked me to spell it. After I finished she looked thoughtful for a moment and then asked, "Would it be helpful do you think to question any of the other students Miss Williams was tutoring?" She was certainly skipping around.

"I don't know." Ron was frowning. "I never saw any of them except for a couple of times she asked me to help her make some tea and sandwiches for them. My father's expertise was a big help there, of course," he added, giving me a quick wink.

"I feel there are two steps we may take immediately," Aunt Kay was saying. "You have a key to Miss Williams' residence. Tomorrow you will go there, ostensibly to clean as your job requires. Only you will clean out anything which strikes you as odd, unusual, anything out of place, anything which strikes your imagination. And you will bring those articles back here to me.

Secondly, we will try an ad in the personal columns of the various newspapers in town. In the largest possible typeface:

IMPORTANT AND VITAL INFORMATION
ABOUT NIOBE
PLEASE CONTACT IMMEDIATELY
AT – –

give this phone number. Do you have that, Lisa?"

I did and said so.

"Then that was important?" Ron exclaimed, brightening. "I was afraid you'd think I was crazy."

"On the contrary, it is quite suggestive. Niobe was a character in Greek mythology whose pride cost her her children and who was turned into stone, in which state she still wept for the loss."

"But Miss Williams didn't have any children — " I began, but Ron cut me off with his own protest.

"Mrs. Farraday, I can't see that we have *any* information, much less important and vital — "

"Mr. Van Cleave. If I am to help, you will have to trust in my judgement. Long experience has taught me that in seeking information it is best to let the party with the information assume that you, too, have some to exchange. Besides, the way the advertisement is worded does not indicate whether we want to give or receive."

She let out a deep sigh. "Well, it is getting late and I feel we have done all that is possible in a first meeting. In all candor I am not overly optimistic about the success our first two exploratory probes will ultimately bring us. However, there are few avenues open to us."

28

She extended her hand. Ron took it and thanked her. He tried to bring up the subject of payment again but Aunt Kay waved it away.

"For now I do not require a retainer. We will turn the advertisement bill over to you for payment. After that we shall see. I assure you that my eventual bill will be commensurate with my efforts . . . I mean, *our* efforts."

That was when he finally turned to me.

"Uh . . . Lisa, want to go someplace for a quick pizza or something?"

As you might imagine, it wasn't merely the fact that I hadn't exactly made a pig of myself over the liver loaf at dinner which made that sound like a great idea to me. As a matter of fact, up until that moment I had begun to wonder if Miss Williams was going to be the only person missing from Ron's life.

"Super!" I told him, forgetting all about the advice I had been silently giving myself not to appear over-eager. "Just give me a sec' to change."

I started for my room, thinking how cool my wrap-around skirt would look with my new halter top, when I was stopped cold by my aunt's voice.

"Unfortunately, Mr. Van Cleave, my 'confidential assistant' must turn down your charming offer. She is so indispensable to me, you see. And, after she types the notice for tomorrow's newspapers, there will be the transcript of our meeting here tonight for her to do. However, when you visit Miss Williams' residence tomorrow I think it would be an advantage to have her along."

Well, that settled that. And to be painfully

honest, I didn't see that Ron boy shed any tears over having our pizza date terminated.

When I came back from seeing him to the door I called a good night in to Aunt Kay, not wanting her to think I was sulking (Though I really felt like it since that transcript bit was a dirty trick. I can't even type and she knows it.) and was halfway to my room when she called again.

"Remind me to phone the Los Angeles County Morgue in the morning, won't you, Lisa? I didn't want to upset your friend further but I think it's a practical first step."

"He didn't seem so upset," I answered, thinking how easily he'd accepted the disappointment of our not sharing gummy mozzarella and chemical pepperoni together.

"No doubt his anguish was tempered by the discovery of new culinary delights to pass along to his father and the other members of the Chevaliers de Bourgogne."

Just the way she said it I knew she knew from the first.

"If you were wise all along that I made that up, how come you invited him in?"

"Because there are two phenomena of the human condition which never cease to intrigue and enthrall me: the ingenuity of the human mind and the blindness of the human heart. Tonight you exhibited more than a fair measure of both."

She should've witnessed the scene at the door. The cutest boy I've ever seen's parting words were: "You were right. It *was* amazing how easy it was to talk to strangers, to somebody you can tell yourself you don't ever have to see again."

Then he shook my hand. "Blindness of the human heart?"

Really. . . .

5.

Ron didn't lose any time getting into the spirit of things. The first thing he said to my "Good morning" when he picked me up bright and early the next day was:

"I've worked out a cover story for you."

"How super," I said.

"I thought you'd like it."

"Yes. Now tell me what you're talking about."

"You." He shook his head in exasperation. "In case anybody comes and finds us searching Miss Williams' house. After all, I can explain what I'm doing there. As your aunt said, I have a key and I'm just doing my regular chores, but what are you doing there with me?"

I had a few ideas of my own on that subject but it seemed a lot more cool to acknowledge his point.

"All right," I said. "What am I doing there?"

"You're my kid sister."

"Great. Just what I always wanted to be. Did that particular inspiration come to you all in one flash or did you stay up all night thinking of it?"

"You've just arrived from back east," he went on, ignoring my sarcasm, "and I took you with me when I went to work because I couldn't leave you all alone in my place in a strange city and everything."

"Of course not. I might get run over by a truck in your bathroom or electrocute myself with my water pik or something."

"You don't have to take that attitude. I'm only trying to be helpful."

"I can tell that," I said. "But since you and I don't look anything alike, much less like brother and sister, maybe we should use something more believable, like a distant cousin, twice removed. Or we could try something really far-out, like your girlfriend. I mean, unless you think that's stretching the limits of credibility too much?"

"It doesn't make any difference to me," he responded blandly. "Whatever you're comfortable with."

I snuck a look at him out of the corner of my eye, trying to see if there was a zinger in there, but he was just looking straight ahead, concentrating on the Sunset Boulevard traffic.

On the freeway ahead the traffic thickened rapidly. We turned off onto a road that led gradually upward through groves of trees and sprawling subdivisions. Ron's old Maverick chugged along slowly, straining even though we weren't really up very far in the hills.

We made a turn and pulled up in front of a small, simple white stucco house on a street of small stucco houses.

We got out and Ron led the way up the path to the front door. He took the precaution, as he'd explained to me that he would, of knocking and ringing. After a decent wait in which there was absolutely no response, he took out his key, opened the door, and motioned me in ahead of him.

We found ourselves standing in a very small foyer. We stood stock still and at first there didn't seem to be any sound at all, but after a second of adjusting from the street noises outside, I could make out a very faint tap-tap-tap sound. It seemed to be coming from somewhere in the back of the house. I started in that direction but Ron grabbed me by the arm.

"Let's make sure," he said. Then, raising his voice, he tried, "Anybody home?" And a little louder, "Miss Williams?" Finally he shouted, "It's Ron Van Cleave!"

Not a sound in response but we made a quick tour just to satisfy ourselves: two bedrooms, bathroom, living room, and kitchen. No sign of life.

In fact, except for some old-fashioned heavy furniture, no sign of anything. It was as if no one had ever lived there.

"Well, we'd better get to it," Ron said. "I traded my morning shift with the guard who usually works evenings but I've still got to work this afternoon."

"It shouldn't take too long," I commented, looking around at the neat little rooms that opened off the foyer.

"No," he agreed, "it's a small house and like

most places out here it doesn't have a cellar or a garage. Different than back home."

I nodded, not wanting to appear too grateful for that little show of empathy.

"I think the most efficient way would be to split it up," I volunteered. "Why don't I take the kitchen, bathroom, and the small bedroom and leave you the two largest rooms. That way it'll sort of even out."

"I guess that's as good a way as any," he said, and walked into the living room.

Actually it wasn't just a random choice. It had occurred to me that being a woman I would be more likely to spot something unusual or out of place in a woman's kitchen or bathroom.

The first thing I did was to clear up the mystery of the tap-tap-tap. It was a leaky faucet in the kitchen. The fact that there was still running water gave me the idea of testing the rest of the utilities. I flicked the light switch in the kitchen and nothing happened. When I picked up the telephone extension on the wall by the stove it was dead too. Which certainly bore out the theory that Miss Emmaline Williams didn't plan to return soon.

My next discovery bore out a different theory or, rather, an additional one; the lady had left in a hurry. As near as I could tell from going through the refrigerator, the shelves, the pantry, and every drawer in the kitchen, all the silverware, plates, dishes, utensils, glasses, and plenty of food had been left behind. It was all neat, everything was in its place, but it didn't seem that anything had been removed. Or, at least, not anything noticeable. Added to the furniture being there, it either meant she was not going to be away for very long, which contradicted Ron, or that she was traveling fast and light. Since we had taken Ron on as our client, I definitely preferred to assume the latter until proven otherwise.

Before I wrote the kitchen off completely, I went over it very carefully with one particular object in mind: any written material that might have been left behind. But aside from a little scrapbook which held a few simple recipes, I drew a total blank in that area. Not even a scrap of paper with a note scrawled on it or a pad of old numbers by the phone.

The bathroom was the same story, only to the nth degree. It had been stripped completely of any and all articles belonging to Miss Emmaline Williams. The medicine chest and the clothes hamper were both bare and the only thing left behind was the shower curtain hanging above the bathtub.

I found Ron in the hall. He was sitting cross-legged on the floor in front of the open closet.

"Any luck?" he asked without looking up.

"Nothing in the bathroom and only standard articles in the kitchen. The only thing I can guess is that she left in a hurry and didn't want to be slowed down carrying food and stuff. I even looked under the paper she used to line the shelves in case there might have been a note or something stuck there and forgotten. *Nada.* How did you make out?"

"About the same. The dresser and night table

36

in the bedroom were empty and all her clothes were gone from the closet."

"*All* her clothes?"

"Let me put it this way, the closet was empty. I don't think Miss Williams was too concerned about clothes anyway. She probably didn't have a lot of them. At least I usually saw her wearing pretty much the same things."

I leaned around him and peered into the open hall closet. There were just a few bare wooden and wire hangers. I leaned in closer and saw what was occupying his attention. There was a stack of magazines on the floor of the closet. They made a pile about a foot high. He had a couple of them spread open.

"You know," he said, still not looking up, "there wasn't anything in the living room either. I went through her desk and the table drawers and most of her books are gone from the bookcase too."

He paused and frowned in a puzzled way.

"I don't see anything strange in that," I said. From all you've said about Miss Williams she's an intellectual lady, a teacher. Naturally her books would be among her most prized possessions and she'd want to take them. Maybe she just couldn't take them all. What kind of car does she drive?"

"A Honda Civic."

"Which is a very small car, right? It all seems to tie together. She just took as many of her things, books or whatever that could fit in a small car."

"What you said about her being an intellectual lady, that's right. Very intellectual. And that's what's bothering me. I was reminded of that when I saw most of her books gone. They were all very heavy reading. She didn't go in for anything light."

He stopped and was staring into the closet again.

"So?"

"So what is a person like Miss Williams, who thought Shakespeare was light entertainment, doing reading stuff like this?"

He gestured to the stack of magazines.

"Well, nobody's completely one-dimensional, Ron. She might have had an occasional light moment."

He shook his head. "Here," he said and pulled the rest of the stack out of the closet. "You take a look at them."

"I see what you mean," I said after riffling through a couple.

They were what have always been referred to, condescendingly, as "women's magazines." And not even the highest quality of those, but the kind of cheaper, trivial ones where the few articles or stories scattered throughout merely provided the padding between pages and pages of glossy advertising for everything from "French perfume" to "authentic Finnish saunas."

"It does seem kind of odd, all right," I conceded. "Especially for a lady who wasn't exactly into trying to be fashionable from everything you've said about her."

"That's not all." He got the magazines together and restacked them.

"The oddest thing about it is that I'm sure

there were a lot more of them. I'd noticed them almost the first time I was here. Only then they were on one of the shelves of the bookcase. Like they meant something to her. And the last time I noticed them, there were about twice as many as there are now. I'm sure of that."

"She must've taken the rest with her."

"That doesn't make it any less strange, does it?" he asked. "For her to leave behind *any* of those books that probably meant so much to her and to take these magazines instead?"

"We don't know that she took them. She might have thrown them out."

"The trash can!" He got to his feet. "I should have thought of that before."

I followed him back to the kitchen and out through the back door.

"That was one of the things I did for her, carry out the trash. The can was too heavy for her to handle."

Out in back alongside a little stoop was a galvanized metal garbage can. Ron picked the lid up and looked in. It was empty.

"It looks just the way I left it the last time I was here. I was hoping we might find something, if not the magazines, at least something that would give us a clue."

"The missing magazines *not* being there might be a clue," I volunteered helpfully. "Besides, its being empty doesn't mean she didn't throw stuff out. Wouldn't the trashmen bring the can back here after they emptied it?"

"No, that's just it, they don't. That was one of my chores. After carrying the can out to the front for collection days, I'd always bring the empty can back the next day from where they left it."

"Then, for what it's worth, we've established that she didn't throw out anything, because even if she had somehow decided to wrestle that can out to the front, she certainly didn't stick around until the next day and bring it back here.

"Well," I continued, thinking out loud while we walked back inside, it seems as if Miss Williams ran out in a hurry."

Ron had stopped in the hall and was standing there looking down at the remaining magazines again. "Maybe she was *taken* out," he said glumly.

"We haven't found any signs of violence," I said, trying to make him feel better. "And Miss Williams did take the time to have the phone and electricity shut off. That hardly seems as if she was struggling for life and limb."

"Anybody could've done that. It just takes a phone call to the power and phone companies."

He looked at his wrist watch. "Why don't you help me go through the books that were left in the bookcase? People sometimes leave notes or even letters between the pages of books."

And no doubt they do. But not Miss Emmaline Williams. I was beginning to think of her as a phantom. She certainly didn't leave many traces of her existence. She not only hadn't left any notes or letter in her books, she hadn't left any marks. I didn't even find a single passage underlined in any of the books I went through. As for the books themselves, I only feel qualified to report that they all dealt with economics and were certainly anything *but* frivolous reading.

"It's getting late and I've got to be back on duty at the pool," Ron said after we'd put the books back on the shelves.

There was no doubt he was pretty down. I trudged dutifully after him in the direction of the front door but once again he halted in front of the closet.

"One thing I did notice about those magazines," I offered, trying to be constructive. "They were all a couple of years old. The ones that you think are missing, did you happen to notice if they went back that far, too?"

"Not really. Except now that you mention it, the ones on top, the only ones I really saw, didn't look as ragged as these here in the closet."

"Then she might have kept them in chronological order. The ones I glanced at are."

"Now that you mention that" — there was a little note of excitement in his voice — "the ones I noticed were fancier, not cheap looking like these."

"You mean like *Vogue*?"

He threw up his hands. "How would I know when it comes to things like that? Forget it, I'm probably just grasping at straws."

But he still just stood there staring dejectedly down at the pathetic little stack of cheap magazines.

"Let's take them, Ron. I really hate to go back to my aunt empty-handed."

"You really think there's a chance they might be important?"

"I don't know," I said in all honesty. "But what I *do* know is that we ought to give Aunt Kay a chance to find out."

Ron didn't need any further urging. He was probably thankful for the opportunity to do anything positive. He scooped them up and out we went, locking the door behind us.

As we drove away I noticed a glass bird feeder at the edge of the front lawn. There was a bird perched there, sipping through the spout.

"We didn't seem to need your elaborate cover story," I said, letting him know, in a playful way, that I hadn't forgotten his original view of me as a fifth wheel.

"Just as well," he commented drily.

Which made me decide to spend the rest of the ride back totally engrossed in the magazines. If he expected any more bright ideas like pretending to be his girlfriend, he'd have to put in a formal request. He'd just have to learn that when I'm working on a case, I'm all business.

6.

Going over the magazines with Aunt Kay turned out to be a long and grueling process. Especially since I only had Ron's assistance for the first hour or so. We didn't even stop for lunch, continuing on through mouthfuls of the sandwiches Mrs. Di brought to us. Right after the last bite of prosciutto, cheese, and sliced tomato on Italian bread (whole-grain Italian bread, Mrs. Di's concession to Aunt Kay's obsession with health food), Ron departed for his afternoon shift at the pool and I struggled on alone. It wasn't just that everything in those magazines had either to be read or described aloud to Aunt Kay, or even her constant questions and interruptions. What made it totally unbearable was the magazines themselves. The endless repetition of (to me, anyway) meaningless, boring fluff.

It was getting close to dinner time when Aunt Kay finally leaned back in her chair and sighed. "I am afraid we are drilling a dry hole."

I was ready to admit that the only value to that

pile of magazines was the chance they'd given me to occupy my mind and ignore Ron on the ride back from Miss Williams' house.

Walking into the dining room, Aunt Kay summed up. "If Miss Williams did take the newer, better quality magazines, as Mr. Van Cleaves surmises, there is no discernible clue as to why, or why such material was apparently important to her or, indeed, why she disappeared at all or where she disappeared to. Not in those magazines. Not to us, at least, with our meagre knowledge of her."

After we were seated, Aunt Kay remarked that she had called the morgue in the morning and that their response to her inquiry was the only negative one so far that we could feel good about.

"Well, I'm glad to hear that," I said, wishing to myself that thoughts of cadavers hadn't been saved for dinner.

Mrs. Di served and then joined us as she often did. Her relationship with Aunt Kay was an informal one, not strictly employer and employee, and when the phone rang in the middle of the main course I told her not to bother, I'd get it. I'd had about all I could take of their eel in green sauce, anyway, and was glad to get away without insulting either of them.

"I'm calling about your advertisement in the paper." The voice in my ear was excited and definitely feminine.

I could feel my heart jump (unless it was the eel) up into my throat. Trying to keep my voice

44

casual, I said, "I see. Would you like an appointment?"

"Could I have your name, please?" I needed a moment to think and that seemed like a proper question to ask.

"My name won't mean anything to you. Look, if you . . . This is important to me. I want to see you right away." There was a pause and then she said, doubtfully, "You sound awfully young."

"It's my aunt whom you'll have your appointment with," I told her with dignity. "Please hold on a minute while I check with her."

Aunt Kay and Mrs. Di were still smacking their lips and devouring eel when I walked back into the dining room.

"There's a lady on the phone about the ad. She wants to see you right away."

"We'll be through with dinner in half an hour," my aunt responded in her usual imperturbable manner.

"Wouldn't it be better to have her come when Ron could be here, too? He might recognize her or — "

"I wish we could afford that luxury, Lisa. But this is our first nibble and if you play out too much line you lose the fish."

"You're the boss," I said and started back for the phone.

"After you hang up, dear, you might get those magazines out of sight."

I told Ms. Anonymous that we'd expect her in half an hour and gave her the name and address.

Actually I wasn't all that sorry Ron wasn't

there to see her when Mrs. Di ushered our mysterious caller into the study thirty minutes later on the dot. She was one dynamite looking lady. And that was without any help. Not a speck of make-up and dressed in baggy jeans and a nondescript top. She was tall, with long auburn hair, and I estimated her age to be not much over twenty-five.

"This is my aunt, Mrs. Farraday," I told her, adding, "of course, I don't know your name."

"My name isn't really important." She had a low, very controlled voice. It struck me as something she'd worked on and, together with her striking features, made me wonder if she might be an actress. In fact there was something vaguely familiar about her and I tried to recall any television shows or movies I'd watched lately to see if her face fit, but nothing specific registered.

My aunt came around from behind her desk, pulled a chair out for herself, and indicated the one that was always there for our caller.

"That is my niece, Lisa Farraday," Aunt Kay said, gesturing to where she knew I'd be sitting. "Also my eyes."

"Oh, I didn't realize . . . ," Ms. Anonymous said and sat.

"Aunt Kay did too, facing her. "Yes, I'm blind. And now that that's out of the way and you see that I am a respectable if slightly decrepit old lady lawyer, perhaps you would care to tell us your name?"

"Perhaps. After you've given me the 'vital and important information' about Niobe."

"Of course. That is what this meeting is for,

after all. However, I must first ask you to establish your *bona fides*."

"My what?"

"Your connection with Niobe. I assume you are not claiming to *be* Niobe yourself. Or are you?"

"No, of course not." There was a hint of the nervousness I'd detected on the phone and she cleared her throat.

Actually, that was pretty clever of my aunt, putting her on the defensive immediately. She told me later that it was the first hint that our caller wasn't exactly sure who Niobe was.

"You said you're a lawyer, Mrs. Farraday? Is the information you have for me of a legal nature?"

"It may well prove to be. Actually, you know, the biggest part of a lawyer's job is to keep matters out of a court of law," Aunt Kay said smoothly. "Oh, please excuse my poor hospitality. We've just finished dinner and I wonder if you'd care for coffee or something with us?"

"No. Thank you."

"You won't object if we do?"

"No. Please go ahead."

I went in to tell Mrs. Di and found that she had it ready and waiting. Coffee for me and a cup of vile-looking herbal tea for my aunt.

". . . so you see it would constitute gross negligence on my part to reveal privileged information under those circumstances," Aunt Kay was saying when I came back in.

"Here's your health glop, Aunt Kay."

"Thank you, dear. I was just telling our guest that I should, by all rights, have both her name

47

and her connection with Niobe. However, in the interests of time, I am willing to waive one." She turned to the mystery lady. "Which shall it be?"

For one horrible second I thought Ms. Anonymous was going to jump up and scoot. Her gaze did flicker toward the door. Then she composed herself.

"Very well. I don't seem to have any choice. If you're an attorney . . ." She dug into a pocket and took out a wallet.

"Here's fifty dollars. If I retain you as my attorney, anything I tell you will be privileged and confidential, right?"

"I admire your prudence, but unfortunately I already have a client, and since there is always a chance of conflicting interests, I can't accept a retainer from you. However, you may rely on our discretion. Always assuming, of course, that you have not committed a felony," Aunt Kay went on in her best prosecutor's tone.

"No, no, it's nothing like that. At least I don't think it is."

She took a deep breath. "First, I should tell you that I grew up in a foster home. I never knew who my mother and father were or even if they were alive. I was placed in an institution as a baby and adopted when I was three. That's one reason I don't want you to know my real name. My foster parents are, well, they're really nice and they did their best and . . . well, I'd just as soon leave them out of this."

"As I said that will be acceptable as long as you state your connection with Niobe in full."

"Full?" She laughed without any humor. "I'm

48

afraid it's not very full." She paused and cleared her throat again.

"A few days ago I received a sealed envelope in the mail with no return address. When I opened it there was a key and a brief, typewritten note. The note consisted of the name and address of a bank and the number of a safety deposit box which it said would be in my name. Needless to say, I was curious and went to the bank the next day. Inside the safety deposit box was a handwritten note and a great deal of money. One hundred and forty three thousand dollars to be exact. My connection with Niobe is that is how the letter was signed."

She stopped as if that was all she was going to say so Aunt Kay prodded. "And what did that mean to you? Personally, apart from the money, I mean?"

"Well, nothing. Of course I looked up Niobe and found she was a myth — "

"That's not what I meant, as you well know. Do you have the letter with you?"

"No."

"My dear young lady, why prolong this by assuming that I am obtuse? A letter to you signed 'Niobe' could only have come from your natural mother. Now that we have established that, it is time for candor on your part."

"I can tell you what the letter said. It was very brief. It stressed that I was not illegitimate and apologized for giving me away. It said that someday she hoped to be able to tell me her reasons personally but that for now she hoped the money would be some small compensation and consolation for what she was not equipped to give me."

"And how did she account for that rather substantial sum?"

"What makes you think she did? Why should she have to?"

"Surely the source is pertinent? I doubt it was available at your birth. Rich fairy princesses are only abandoned in fairy tales."

There was another pause and then she said, "You mentioned you already have a client. Who is it?"

"My client's name would mean no more to you than your name would to me," said Aunt Kay with a glint in her eye.

"But you do know Niobe's name, don't you?" the young woman came back like a shot.

I was surprised at Aunt Kay. I didn't think she could be bluffed so easily. I had already figured out that Miss Williams was probably her mother but I made an effort not to let it show. Poor old Aunt Kay, however, blew her cool completely. She actually trembled and lost control of the cup of herbal tea. If our mystery guest hadn't caught it the tea would have spilled right into her lap. As it was, some of it slopped over her hands.

"I do beg your pardon. I'm not usually so clumsy. Lisa, fetch a tissue or something, please."

"Don't bother. It's all right." Ms. Anonymous set the cup down on the desk, produced a tissue from her pocket, and wiped her hands. "You still haven't answered my question," she said.

"Before I could divulge your mother's name,

you would have to produce the letter. And, if you're thinking of a spot of forgery, let me warn you that we are in a position to authenticate Niobe's handwriting."

"I'll just bet you are." The voice wasn't so controlled now and it also made you realize why she controlled it. It was hard.

"Will you produce the letter?"

"You're very good at asking for things but not so good at answering." She stood up. "You know what I think? I think you're fishing. I think *you're* looking for that 'vital and important information.' I think it's my father who's your — "

She stopped suddenly as if afraid she'd gone too far. "What I really think is I was a fool to tell you as much as I have." She turned and strode gracefully from the room. I went to the door but she was already through it ahead of me, and all that was left for me to do was to lock it behind her.

Back in the study, I found Aunt Kay rummaging around in her desk.

"I didn't think she'd split so fast. Do you think you should have told her? I mean, it's obvious Miss Williams is her mother."

"I don't believe in giving information away for nothing. It was also obvious that young woman had told us all she was going to tell us tonight."

Aunt Kay had a pencil in her hand as she joined me in front of the desk.

"No, I'm afraid that had we told her, she would have thanked us sweetly and shown us her heels even sooner. It was necessary to keep her on edge, keep her guessing." She extended the pencil in my direction. "Please take hold of that cup by the handle and bring it in to Mrs. DiPasquale, will you, Lisa?"

"No need to bother her. I can wash our cups out myself."

"You may wash *your* cup if you so desire, but please hold mine with this pencil. Mrs. DiPasquale is waiting."

"What are you talking —" I glanced down at the cup. "You didn't even drink any of it?"

"I have never acquired a taste for ink. However, it does do nicely for fingerprints."

"Oh," I said and did as I was told.

When I returned, Aunt Kay was back behind her desk and I recognized the expression on her face as one she assumed whenever she wanted to be left alone to think.

"Excuse me," I said. "I hate to interrupt in case you're thinking up another number that you can spring without telling me so that I feel like a fool, but I thought maybe this would be a good time to go over what we found out tonight?"

She jerked her head around as if she had forgotten I was there and then asked, "Can you get your Mr. Van Cleave here?"

"Well, the pool's closed but I could call him at home and —"

"No. The morning will do. You might as well go to bed."

"But I thought —"

"Thought will be my department tonight. We must proceed on the assumption that her letter contains some clue to Miss Williams' whereabouts. Unfortunately, that young woman is playing a game of her own, whatever it may be. I only hope our tactics don't backfire and drive her to do something foolish."

"You think she may be in danger?"

"I don't know. Confound it, I don't know anything. How could I when the only clue we have is a letter we can't get a hold of? But something made Miss Williams flee! Collect your impressions of this young woman tonight and tell them to me tomorrow. Remember you are my eyes."

Obviously, logical argument is pointless with a person who says, "thought is my department." I smiled my mature, self-possessed smile and retired to my room. Only to wake in the middle of the night dreaming of a beautiful woman who forged portraits of lifeguards, fingerpainting them from cups of ink.

7.

By the time Ron could get away from the pool it was lunch time and I was half out of my head with frustration over not being able to discuss the night before with Aunt Kay. She was still shut up in the study and had even left orders not to let me take her breakfast tray in.

"When your friend comes," Mrs. Di had said, backing through the study door and holding the tray of tea, toast, and eggs so that it projected out in front of her stomach like a shelf, "your Great Aunt Catharine told me that she'll go over everything with the both of you then."

So I had chewed my nails and waited. But Aunt Kay was not only as good as her word, she didn't waste any time on formalities. No sooner had Mrs. Di seated Ron at the table, than Aunt Kay glided silently in and fired her opening salvo.

"Mr. Van Cleave, we had a development yesterday evening after you had left. I have kept Lisa on pins and needles ever since. Partly due to the idiosyncratic nature of my thought processes and also to spare myself the necessity of repeating my deductions all over again to you, once you joined us here."

She sat and Mrs. Di started serving our lunch — a French Mediterranean casserole of eggplant, tomatoes, zucchini, onion, and cauliflower, topped and baked with cheese.

"It cost me a night's sleep and Lisa is ready to jump out of her skin so I'll not beat around the bush. Do you know what bank Miss Williams did business with?"

"Well, I know one," Ron answered easily. "Maybe there were others, but the couple of times she paid me by check they were drawn on the First Industrial Bank & Trust Co."

"That's a big bank. Do you remember which branch?"

"Sure. The main office in Century City. That's how come I remember the bank at all. I needed cash right away once and that's where I had to go to cash it."

My aunt turned to me. "Lisa, there's a Directory of American Banking on the bookshelf next to the Blackstones. Please bring it while I fill Mr. Van Cleave in on what transpired last night."

I headed for the study while Aunt Kay began by telling Ron how the magazines had been a wash-out but the ad had drawn blood.

The Directory of American Banking turned out to be a big, heavy book. No doubt the kind that Miss Emmaline Williams would enjoy. Just to make sure, I looked through it until I came to a listing for the First Industrial Bank & Trust Co., before lugging it into the dining room.

"Turn to where their Board of Directors and officers are listed. The name you're looking for is Harold Crosswell," Aunt Kay said, and then went back to describing our meeting with the mystery woman to Ron.

I wanted to be absolutely positive before admitting defeat, so I went over that list of names three times before facing up to another dead end. By then Aunt Kay had finished briefing Ron and he was looking hopefully in my direction. Which didn't make it any easier.

"I'm sorry, Aunt Kay, there isn't any Harold Crosswell listed. Not here."

Aunt Kay, however, hung tough. "Hmmmmm," she hmmmmed, "Sometimes I do lose track of other people's ages in my determination not to pay any attention to my own. Poor old Harry must be seventy-five if he's a day and long since forced into retirement if I know banks." She made a face. "Now that he knows more about banking and corporate finance than any man on the west coast, their brilliant idea is to put him out to pasture, thereby weakening themselves and killing him."

She shook her head. "Very well, there's nothing we can do about it. Read *all* the names listed there please, Lisa."

I did. Starting with the Board of Directors. I had just begun to work my way through the officers when Aunt Kay requested a repeat.

"Bertram W. Gulden, Executive Vice-President," I said again.

"Bert Gulden." Aunt Kay nodded, a smile creasing the worry lines in her face. "It's high time something clicked. Bert Gulden arranged the financing for most of my husband's pictures," she explained to us.

She finished the helping of casserole that was on her plate before continuing. "Of course we are proceeding on the assumption that Miss Williams is Niobe and that the one hundred forty-three thousand dollars not only exists, but came from her, and that a sum of such magnitude left a trail, the first traces of which may be found at her bank. Naturally, banks are reluctant to divulge information of this sort, of any sort, in my opinion, but presumably an Executive Vice-President will be able to override objections of procedure or ethics or whatever. The success of Jack's pictures did nothing to impede Mr. Bert Gulden's rise in the world of banking, and if he is still as grateful as he once said he was, I shall attempt to impose on that gratitude."

"Excuse me," Ron interrupted. "But aren't you doing just what you said you wouldn't do? Beating around the bush? Wouldn't it have been better to go directly through this woman who answered the ad? You say she's Miss Williams' daughter! Well, I can't believe that for one minute. But, for the sake of argument, say that she knows something. Why didn't you show her that we are on her side? Tell her the truth? Get her to work together with us? Then you wouldn't have to go cooking up some complicated scheme with this bank."

"Because instinct told me that young woman has fish of her own to fry." Aunt Kay wasn't fazed. "Which leads me to the theory that I want

57

you two to explore. Hopefully, with the aid of Mr. Gulden."

"That the money came from the father? Or at least some of it?" I couldn't help blurting it out. I'd been holding it in for so long. "Is that what you figured too?"

Aunt Kay allowed herself a smile in my direction. "Sometimes, Lisa, I think there's still hope for your brain."

Ron was shaking his head. "I just can't imagine Miss Williams accepting money from a man who supposedly fathered her child and then took off. She's just too proud. Too independent."

"We don't know that *he* took off. Maybe she was the one who ended the relationship." I had to get that in. Men like to think that they have the exclusive franchise for dumping.

"And don't forget," I added, "her letter was emphatic about them being married."

"If there even *is* any such letter." Ron wasn't going to give in easily. "Why couldn't that woman have made up all or any part of her story?"

"What would she gain by such a fabrication?" Aunt Kay was shaking her head. "Besides, the wording she quoted had an authentic ring to it. I am thinking particularly of the phrase about not being 'equipped' to take care of a child. I heard that young woman talk and she is incapable of inventing a phrase like that. But intuitively I feel that Miss Williams would be comfortable with it. It seems to me entirely possible that Miss Williams is the mother of that young woman and, of course, supplied the one hundred forty-three thousand dollars."

Ron was silent for a moment. "It's just that . . ." He finally said, "It's as if you're saying that Miss Williams would . . . well . . . blackmail the father. I mean, where else would she get so much money?"

"It doesn't have to be blackmail, does it?" I was teed off. "Why can't men imagine women acquiring money any other way but through sex or trickery?" I also couldn't imagine a woman who was dedicated to helping kids being a blackmailer. "You weren't thinking of blackmail, were you Aunt Kay?"

"Actually dear, blackmail was precisely what I had been thinking of."

Ron shook his head in disgust. For a second I thought he was going to get up and storm out like our mystery lady of the night before.

"But not by Miss Williams." Aunt Kay was continuing, obviously thinking it out as she went along. "Think back, Lisa. When that young woman lost her temper, when she felt that she had been tricked by us and then tried to accuse us of the worst motive she could think of, what accusation did she make? Being in league with her father!"

"That's right."

"It all comes back to the letter," said Aunt Kay. "It might just have informed her that her natural father was the source of the money. But without naming him."

"*If* he was." I put my two cents in again.

"You mean you think that *she* might be planning to blackmail her real father?" Ron's face

59

showed disbelief. "That would take a pretty slimy person."

"Who can calculate the hurt and resentment which smolder in the breast of a child abandoned, placed in an institution, shunted to foster parents?"

"You know, Aunt Kay, she didn't seem to feel very close to her foster parents either, did she? She didn't seem to think they were capable of understanding her." For the first time I tried to imagine how I would feel if that had happened to me. Awful as things sometimes get at home, I couldn't even imagine the horror of being abandoned as a baby. The ultimate rejection. All at once I felt terribly sorry for that incredibly beautiful lady.

"I only hope we have aroused that young woman's curiosity enough to get her to come back," Aunt Kay sighed. "We must have that letter." She pushed her chair back from the table. "I think it's time I called Bert Gulden."

In the study I reminded her about the fingerprints.

"Mrs. DiPasquale took them downtown before you got up this morning. Mr. Phillips at the Attorney General's office was most generous. Both in his remembrance of the times I opposed him years ago in court and in his promise to have an answer for us as soon as possible."

8.

The executive offices of the First Industrial Bank & Trust Co. were on the third floor. Their private elevator lifted us, smoothly and soundlessly, from the austere, modernistic lobby up into an atmosphere of elegant simplicity.

"I guess this is all designed to give these executive types the impression that they're rising effortlessly to an exalted level above the crowd," Ron commented sarcastically as we stepped out.

A lady with very blonde hair nodded when I told her who we had come to see and repeated our names into the intercom on her desk.

Mr. Gulden didn't look as old as I had expected. Even though his thick, wavy hair was all white, the contrast it made with his deeply tanned face somehow created an illusion of youth. Or maybe that was due to his forceful, hearty manner.

After shaking hands with us both, he ushered us into his large office and went through the usual amenities and polite, fond recollections of

Aunt Kay and Uncle Jack. Then he asked us exactly what we expected of him.

"Your Great Aunt Catharine was a little vague on the phone."

"Aunt Kay is very discreet," I said, figuring that would make Brownie Points with a banker.

I explained about Miss Williams' disappearance and the money and that we just wanted to see if it had come from her bank. Aunt Kay had rehearsed me so that the story would give the impression that she was actually acting on behalf of Ron. Aunt Kay had said that would make things go more smoothly, giving us a kind of official status in our investigation.

She was right. That, and what Mr. Gulden called Aunt Kay's "impeccable track record for probity" (I have since looked up *probity* in the dictionary and found it means "complete uprightness in one's dealings") finally overcame his natural banker's caution.

"It shouldn't be any problem," he said. "All it will take is some digging. Everything is computerized today, you know." He hesitated. "I wouldn't feel right just turning it over to a clerk, though." He was staring down at the top of his desk. "I think I know just the lad for you." He looked up, beaming. He was the kind of person who could use words like "lad" without sounding stagey.

"Come with me," he ordered, and we followed him out of his office, turning the other way, away from the elevators, through a door and down a flight of stairs.

"Bruce is a kind of protégé of mine, you might say," he did say and led us through another door.

"Computers — that's the name of the game today," he went on. The corridor we turned onto had thick carpeting and indirect lighting. "No more gut reactions," Mr. Gulden continued. "Nowadays a committee reports its findings, they run it through a computer, and then another committee of analysts makes a report on that."

He stopped in front of a door with lettering that read "Mr. Downley" and knocked once before pushing it open and walking in. He held the door and Ron and I followed.

It was a nice office, nothing as grand as Mr. Gulden's but tastefully decorated. On the walnut desk was a bowl of freshly cut flowers. The prints that hung on the oak walls picked up the colors of the flowers and cheered up the room.

Mr. Downley couldn't have been out of his twenties, with dark hair and a tan which was even deeper than Mr. Gulden's. His legs, encased in form-fitting English flannels, were stretched out, crossed at the ankles, and resting on top of a pile of ledgers that teetered up from the floor. He was wearing a Madras shirt and there was a beautifully tailored blazer hanging from the back of his chair.

He looked up, saw Mr. Gulden, gave him a dazzling smile, and then extended it to Ron and me, gesturing toward some chairs placed haphazardly around the room.

We all sat. Mr. Gulden leaned across to us, saying in a low voice: "Bruce Downley's the brightest of this new breed. Corporate analysis.

Very scientific. Got all the answers, don't you know. Spotted his potential right away, if I do say so myself."

The subject of those remarks was talking into the phone:

"They'll scream, Pete, but they won't bleed, believe me. As soon as there's enough feedback, you hook me right into the program and it's all circuits 'go.' Right. Talk to you then."

He hung up and swiveled to face us.

"Bruce," said Mr. Gulden, "I want you to meet the grandniece of an old friend of mine, Lisa Farraday. And her friend, Ron Van Cleave. This is Mr. Downley."

"Bruce," he said, shaking Ron's hand but smiling at me.

"Bruce." I acknowledged and found myself smiling back. It was easy to see why Mr. Gulden had spotted his potential right away. I did.

"What can I do for you?" He had moved the smile back to Mr. Gulden.

"Something in the nature of a personal favor. Ordinarily I wouldn't take up your time with what amounts to nothing more challenging than a clerical chore. But I hope you'll humor me and make the time to help these young people."

"Well, naturally, I'd be glad to help you out with anything, Mr. Gulden."

Mr. Gulden turned to me. "Why don't you tell Bruce about your missing teacher? Bruce, you'll see that there isn't anyone else I could trust with something I want to keep confidential. This matter may be small, but it is delicate."

Mr. Gulden was still hearty and affable and all but there must have been a tone of command in his words because suddenly Bruce Downley's whole attitude changed. He really listened to everything I told him and I could see from his face that there was no question about his helping.

"I see," was his only comment when I'd finished. He looked from me to Mr. Gulden. "I'll make the time of course."

"That's fine." Mr. Gulden looked at his wrist watch. "I have a committee meeting in half an hour. I'll just leave you all together to work out the details, if you don't mind. It was a pleasure to meet you, Lisa and Ron. Give my warmest regards to your aunt and tell her she'll hear from me just as soon as Bruce reports." He waved and was gone.

I went over all the information we needed from Bruce Downley, stressing the possibility of a safety deposit box, but that it would be in someone else's name even though Miss Williams would have paid for it. Ron added a couple of things, Bruce had a few questions, the answers to which he wrote down, and I racked my brain but couldn't think of anything we hadn't covered.

"As I understand it," Bruce summed up finally, "the essential point at issue here is to see if we at the bank have a record of your Mrs. — what's her name again?" He fumbled through the copious notes he had made.

"Williams," Ron told him. "Miss or Ms. Emmaline Williams. I spelled it before, you might remember," he added a little touchily.

"Right." Bruce let the dig pass. "And this Miss Williams made deposits totaling somewhere in the neighborhood of one hundred and forty three thousand dollars. And you want to trace the money, if possible, right?"

"Yes, and also the safety deposit box," I reminded him.

"I hadn't forgotten anything you've said," he smiled.

I looked at Ron. "Anything else you can think of?" He shook his head.

"Well," said Bruce, "then I think that's it for now. The ball seems to be in my court."

We thanked him and he took my hand to shake goodbye.

"Try to bear with me," was his parting remark. "Don't think I'm not aware of what this must mean to you, but Mr. Gulden has an embarrassingly generous tendency to exaggerate on my behalf. I'm really just a very small frog in this very big pond."

Down in the parking lot, waiting for Ron to unlock his car, I thought I'd compliment him on the suggestions he'd made.

"That was really neat that you thought to ask him to look for any record they might have of checks drawn on other banks, especially out-of-town banks. They could be a tremendous help in finding Miss Williams."

"It was obvious. She's disappeared, why not to some place she'd been before? If she used a bank there . . . well, it was worth a shot."

"It's a great idea."

"'Deep Tan' didn't seem to think so."

"Who?" I asked, raising my brows and trying not to look too superior.

"The genius."

"Oh. Bruce, you mean?" I asked innocently. "I'm sure he appreciated it. Probably the only reason he didn't show more enthusiasm is that it means all the more work for him."

"Sure. That's understandable. He needs every spare minute he can get for surfing or paddleball or whatever he does to get that tan."

"Mmmmmmmm," I agreed, still all innocence. "He does seem to be in great shape."

"I didn't notice," came the haughty response.

"Just as well," I said, giving him a taste of his own medicine, remembering how he'd pulled that on me when we were leaving Miss Williams' house. Only this time he would be the one to do the thinking on the ride back.

9.

When Ron popped in unexpectedly the next day before we'd even had breakfast, I admit I did allow myself a secret little inner smile. Not a full gloat, just a small grin. There is nothing, I told myself, like a taste of jealousy to restore the proper balance to a male-female relationship.

And it was perfectly harmless, that was the best part. I hadn't done any manipulating; it was all in Ron's head. In fact, he really should have known better. I mean it should have been obvious that I wouldn't be interested in anyone as old as Bruce Downley. Of course it was true that Bruce had paid quite a lot of attention to me but I was too level-headed to blow that up out of proportion.

"I have a week's vacation coming to me," Ron said as soon as he walked into what my aunt calls the sitting room.

Mrs. Di had shown him in and she was still standing alongside. "Shall I set another place for breakfast?" she asked.

My aunt said yes, but Ron said, "Thanks, but I already ate. Listen." He advanced farther into the room as Mrs. Di went back to the kitchen. "I'm trying to tell you. I gave them notice down at the office that I'm taking my vacation now. Starting today. That way I'll have all my time free to help find Miss Williams."

"We're going to need all the help we can get the way things are going, I'm afraid." Aunt Kay got to her feet. "I was just about to tell Lisa of the latest development. Or, rather, nondevelopment. We might as well all discuss it over breakfast. I'm sure a growing young man can manage something? A cup of coffee at least?"

"Sure. Thank you." Ron looked at me but I was just as much in the dark as he was about what my aunt was going to reveal.

By the time we'd finished eating, Ron's "cup of coffee, at least" had become a good sized portion of Mrs. Di's Mexicali omelette of peppers, onions, mushrooms, and two kinds of cheese, together with her home-made sausage and half a loaf of her own genuine sour-dough bread, toasted and smeared lavishly with butter.

Aunt Kay began by telling us that she'd heard from her friend Mr. Phillips of the Attorney General's office.

"Unfortunately there is no record of that young woman's fingerprints. Not here, or at the state capitol in Sacramento, or even in the Central Fingerprint File of the Federal Bureau of Investigation in Washington which has over fifty million prints, completely computerized."

69

"Is she now another dead end?" Ron was upset. "Is that what that means?"

"It means that she has never been arrested for a felony, served in the armed forces, or worked at certain jobs where, by law, employees are fingerprinted."

"What jobs, Aunt Kay? I told you she seemed like an actress to me. At least she was very stagey."

"And attractive, from your description." Aunt Kay poured herself another cup of tea. "There was also something suggestive in the way she hesitated when she referred to her name. And at one point she used the phrase "my real name." In thinking about it I have come to the conclusion that she uses a professional name, or at least a name different from that of her foster parents. And certainly different from the one she was born with."

"All that seems to fit in with her being an actress," I offered.

"I was hoping we might have a stroke of good fortune and find that she'd done some work in a cabaret, and since cabaret licenses require fingerprints, it would have shown up when Mr. Phillips checked for us."

"But the fact that it didn't doesn't rule out the possibility of her being an actress, does it?" I asked. I was positive I had seen that striking face somewhere before.

"No, of course not," Aunt Kay agreed.

"No matter what you, I mean, we try nothing ever seems to come together." Ron's voice sounded very dejected.

"Things never *come* together, Mr. Van Cleave." Aunt Kay was very crisp. "We have to *tie* them together. We make the connections and fashion the knots."

"But all this time Miss Williams may be in danger."

"But this is no time to panic." I felt I had to say something. "We don't know she's in danger, right, Aunt Kay?"

"And we sure don't know she isn't," Ron shot right back. "In fact we don't know *any*thing. How can we when we're always on the defensive, always sitting around waiting for something to happen?"

Well I knew he was depressed and all, but even so, that wasn't fair, and I was just about to tell him what I thought of his making remarks like that when Aunt Kay (who seems to have some kind of psychic power where my thoughts are concerned) smiled and held up a hand to stop me.

"Lisa, Mr. Van Cleave's impatience is understandable. And I sympathize. Your generation is a victim of television. Of quick, slam-bang, simplistic solutions to every problem, no matter how complicated. But unfortunately this is not television and I am not Perry Mason. Nor will car chases or karate chops help to find Miss Williams."

"But what will?" Ron went on doggedly. "You let this woman you think is her daughter get away without finding out anything."

"When we hear from Mr. Gulden at the

bank — " I started to remind him. But he just went right on, ignoring me.

"You don't even know if she really got a letter. Suppose, for argument's sake, that there is a daughter, okay? That ties in with the Niobe thing, I admit. But suppose the woman who came to see you is just somebody posing as the daughter?"

"Even if she was just posing, and I don't credit that for one minute, she's still the best lead we have." Aunt Kay's tone was brisk.

"Right, I agree." Ron wasn't letting go either. "She's a better lead than supposed bank accounts or supposed safety deposit boxes or fingerprints or old magazines or — "

"That's it!" I realized I'd practically jumped right out of my chair. Ron turned and was staring open-mouthed at me and even Aunt Kay looked a bit startled.

"I knew I'd seen her somewhere. I thought it was acting, but when you said that about posing!"

"What are you talking about? What's 'it'?" The look on his face was really infuriating. "Stop babbling and tell us, if you've really got something."

I ignored him and told my aunt. "It was the mention of posing and the magazines practically in the same breath. Otherwise I might still not have made the connection."

"Of course." Aunt Kay was nodding her head, her lips a thin, straight line. "How unimaginative of me. When you were going through the magazines for me, I asked you only about the articles and stories, concerning myself only with the *content*. I excluded — "

"The ads!" I finished the thought for her. I was too excited to wait and this time I did jump off my chair. "I'll get them," I said and streaked out of the dining room and right back with the whole pile of them under my arm. I let Ron help spread them out on the table, being too big to carry a grudge.

It turned out to be easy, the first easy thing so far in the whole affair. I'd only turned a couple of pages of the magazine on top of the first pile before I came right to her. There she was, our Mystery Woman, staring out at me from an advertisement for lingerie. Ron was leaning in and peering over my shoulder.

"Here." I slid half the pile over in front of him. "You might as well go through some of them yourself."

"Yes," Aunt Kay agreed. "We should test the hypothesis thoroughly."

Which didn't take long either. By the time Aunt Kay called a halt to the search we were halfway through the two piles and we'd found her over and over, modeling everything from perfume to pajamas.

"There is no doubt that we have established the basis for your Miss Williams saving these magazines." Aunt Kay addressed herself to Ron. "Of course, on the question of the absolute connection, the identification of the young woman in the advertisements as the same young woman who called on us here, you will have to take our word since you were not present. Do you?"

"Huh? Oh, sure."

"Do you still have doubts as to the relationship between Miss Williams and the woman as understood by my assistant and I?" Aunt Kay's tone was very official.

"Well . . . no." Ron was a little taken aback. "Not really."

I loved it. Aunt Kay was letting him know what she thought of his doubting us. In a businesslike way, of course. After all, he was our client.

"To tie up loose ends," Aunt Kay continued, "Miss Williams obviously kept an eye on her daughter from afar even after she had given her up. The magazines show that she knew of her daughter's career as a model. Her parental pride also accounts for the missing magazines, the ones you described as of better quality and more recent date. She took those with her and left behind the older less impressive ones."

"It's really sad, isn't it?" I said out loud what had been going through my mind. "To imagine that poor lady sitting there month after month, year after year, with only these pictures to comfort her instead of the flesh and blood, *her* flesh and blood, that she must have missed so terribly."

Aunt Kay was thoughtful. "Perhaps," she said. "On the other hand, from all we have learned about Miss Williams, it is hard to imagine her being very comfortable with, or receptive to, the often annoying processes by which the infant human biped makes its needs and desires known."

She shook her head. "Not all women are suited

74

for motherhood, as your Miss Williams was sensible enough to understand, though not prudent enough to avoid."

Ron had picked up another of the magazines and was leaning in toward me again. "Almost as hard to imagine as Miss Williams being a mother," he declared, "is your not recognizing somebody who looks like this." He snapped his finger against the page. It was one of her lingerie advertisements. "I mean, she's really incredibly beautiful," he kept going on. "She'd stand out anywhere."

"She just somehow looked different with her clothes on, I guess, Ron," I answered sweetly.

"Besides," Aunt Kay cut in, "from Lisa's description of her that night, she wore no make-up and was dressed casually, almost dowdily. Isn't that right?"

"Yes," I agreed. "Not the way a model would look at all."

Aunt Kay nodded. "It's certainly not illogical for a woman who earns her bread by posturing and primping, trussed up like a clothes horse and oiled and caked with cosmetics all day long, to eschew such artifices on her own time."

"Okay," I agreed. "That seems to fit. Now that we have a psychological profile of Ms. X the Mystery Model where do we go from there?"

"I can help with the next step, I think," Ron said, coming alive at the prospect of making a positive contribution.

"My father and his ad agency in New York," he reminded us. "He should be able to find out her name. Or at least the name she uses professionally and her address and phone number. All I have to do is phone him and give him the product from one of her ads — I guess it should be the most recent one we have — and the issue and magazine. Advertising is such a small world. They'll know which agency handles that product and he'll get in touch with them and they'll have a record of everybody who was involved in making that ad. I know that from the times on my vacations that I worked there, filling in at his agency."

My aunt wasn't saying anything and Ron stopped abruptly and looked questioningly, first at her and then at me and then back to her.

"Uh . . . is that all right? Is there anything wrong with — "

"No," Aunt Kay answered him. "It's all just fine. Just fine."

10.

Summer afternoons are long and hot in Southern California and my Great Aunt Catharine would prefer to spend them in the coolness of her study listening to the stereo. She has an incredible set of recordings of plays and poetry and even complete novels read by really good actors, and she'd rather listen than read in braille.

That's what she would prefer to be doing. What she was actually doing was spending the afternoon in the coolness of her study asking Ron polite questions about his father's advertising agency.

It was also a way to pass the time while we waited for the call back to Ron from New York, hopefully with the information Ron had requested.

I was in the kitchen, having promised to put Aunt Kay's recipe file in order, when the phone rang. Ordinarily, filing recipes would be a task for Mrs. Di, but I had volunteered just to have something to occupy my mind with. I suppose

I should confess that a small factor in my volunteering was the way Ron had off-handedly rejected my suggestion that he and I go to my room and listen to the new album I'd just bought.

I was still searching intently for a nice tasty recipe for toadstool stew that I could serve him the next time he dropped in when, as I said, the phone rang. There's an extension on the wall near the stove and I picked up the receiver.

"Hello. This is Mrs. Farraday's office."

Since we began working on Ron's case I had been a little unsure as to how to answer the phone, figuring that a confidential assistant should say more than just "hello."

"This is Bertram Gulden," said the hearty voice on the other end.

"Hi, Mr. Gulden. This is Lisa. Did you find anyth — "

"How are you, my dear? Would you put your aunt on, please? Tell her I just got the information she sent you down for."

"Just a sec', I'll get her."

You can imagine what a pleasure it was to interrupt the proceedings in the study. As I entered, Ron was in the middle of a long, drawn out explanation of how they film television commercials at his father's agency. I strolled casually across his line of vision and made my announcement to Aunt Kay.

"Yes, Mr. Gulden," Aunt Kay said into the phone on her desk. There was a pause and then she said, "I see. No, that's most helpful. Yes. I follow your thinking there. Of course."

Another pause and then Aunt Kay said very

quickly, "I'm sure that was the case. I hope you will express my gratitude to Mr. Downley. I really am very grateful for your help and I know I'm also expressing the feelings of my young client."

A third pause and then, "I wonder if it would be possible to impose further on your kindness and generosity? You mentioned an original check?"

Aunt Kay had taken out a pad and was scribbling furiously on it. She held it up so I could see and I managed to make out the barely legible printed scrawl: "TURN ON WALL SWITCH."

Well, looking around, there was one right behind me and I gave it a flick just as I heard Aunt Kay ask Mr. Gulden to go over the first part of the information again. I glanced over to Ron but, if anything, he looked more in the dark even than I was.

"Thank you," Aunt Kay was saying, "I have that all straight now. What I was particularly wondering was how much could be found out about that original check? The one she started the savings account with so many years ago? Yes . . . I appreciate that, naturally . . . no, I was thinking more in the line of who signed it?"

Then there followed the longest pause of all. It was finally broken by a chuckle from Aunt Kay.

"No, Bert, it won't be necessary to produce the signatory on a silver platter. If your intrepid Mr. Downley can produce the name that will be sufficient. Of course, the bank it was drawn on would be better than nothing. Needless to say,

79

I'll be waiting with baited breath. Goodbye, Bert."

She hung up the phone and faced us.

"That switch activates an automatic recording device on this phone, Lisa. For future reference. One of the handicaps of not being able to see. I couldn't take notes and I doubt if Mr. Gulden would put this information in writing. According to what Mr. Downley found out for him there were a series of deposits made by Miss Emmaline Williams over the past nineteen years. I think I remember the pertinent details but of course we'll have the tape to refer to later."

She poured herself a glass of water from the pitcher which always stood on her desk and which Mrs. Di filled twice a day like clockwork. She drank almost the entire glass before continuing.

"They were always made by check from another party, not one of her own. And they were at irregular intervals, but with never less than six months separating each one. The first one was for six thousand dollars. Shortly thereafter all but the minimum balance required to keep the account active was withdrawn. The next deposit was approximately six months later and for a few hundred dollars. That set the pattern for the next nineteen years. The amounts deposited always varied but generally grew gradually larger and larger. The last, which was made only a few days before Miss Williams' disappearance, was by far the largest amount of all, twenty-eight thousand dollars. On the day of your appointment with her which she failed to keep, the day, presumably, on which she disappeared, Miss Williams withdrew the entire contents of her account and closed it. The amount was, of course, one hundred forty-three thousand dollars."

Aunt Kay paused. Ron started to say something, changed his mind, and sat back. I didn't even begin since I knew her pauses were strictly for effect.

"The pattern is suggestive, don't you think?" Aunt Kay was going on. "I asked Mr. Gulden to have your Mr. Bruce Downley find out as much as he could about those checks that Miss Williams deposited with such admirable persistence through the years. Mr. Gulden says that Mr. Downley is getting balky, maintaining that there isn't anything else worth finding out that can be found out, but Mr. Gulden agrees with me that this is just the usual reluctance of somebody who does not stand to gain from work he's doing. Mr. Gulden is sure that by offering Mr. Downley plum assignments in the future, he will soothe his ego and re-awaken his interest in helping us."

Another glass of water, but just a couple of sips this time.

"Of course," she said, "whatever he finds out will just verify what I have already deduced. That all those checks which Miss Williams deposited over the years came from brokerage firms. Stock brokers who buy and sell securities for their customers." Another sip.

"All of the checks but one, that is," she said putting the glass back down. "The original one."

"You asked him especially about that one, didn't you, Aunt Kay? I was wondering why it was important who signed it?"

"When you described that young woman after she had stormed out of here the other night, Lisa, you mentioned to me that you estimated her age at about twenty-five?"

"Yeah, about that, I thought."

"It struck me that the first, the original check with which Miss Williams began her savings account was for six thousand dollars and was deposited nineteen years ago. If your observations of the young woman whom we believe to be Miss Williams' daughter are correct, she was six years old when Miss Williams deposited that first check. Let us just suppose that at that point in time, Miss Williams' path should cross that of the man who was the father of her little girl. And if that man should be compelled to make a financial contribution, for whatever reason, Mr. Van Cleave —"

I had seen Ron start to jump, of course, but how my aunt could tell is beyond me.

"Please do relax," she added. "You have already established yourself as the champion of Miss Williams' moral rectitude. As I was saying, whether from guilt, coercion, or compassion, whatever the impetus, let us say that financial aid was offered. Might not Miss Williams, with her teacher's sense of the fitness of things, with her sense of irony as evidenced by her use of the name 'Niobe,' might not a woman like that demand the exact sum which reflected the life of their child? A thousand dollars for every year she had lived? Lived away and apart from her natural mother. Because she intended that money for the child, and only the child!"

"Yeeees," Ron admitted, nodding his head slowly. "I could see that. I could see her being like that."

"Of course." Aunt Kay obviously had no problem seeing it. "I put myself in Miss Williams' place. What would I do with a windfall of money obtained, by whatever means, from a man who had either scorned me or whom I had scorned? It was inescapable that she couldn't use that money for herself. It would put her in that man's debt, and I know that would be insupportable. She had too much pride."

She paused and that time Ron said, "Yes."

"But to make a game of it! To gamble with it, to treat it as if it meant nothing, that would take the curse off any dependence it might insinuate."

Ron was frowning. "You said the checks came from stockbrokers?" he asked thoughtfully. "I don't understand?"

"The cream of the jest. Or, rather, *gesture*, since it was obviously no joke to your Miss Williams. She would take the money and the opportunity — she had time, years even, before her daughter could use money — to test her own skill, her ability at the one thing which meant the most to her."

"Teaching?" Ron looked really puzzled. "That doesn't make sense."

"No. *What* she taught. By your own testimony, Mr. Van Cleave. Her obsessive interest *in* and knowledge *of* economics. What would a person like that do? Bet on horses? Go to Las Vegas? No, it was inevitable that she would take that six thousand dollars and play the stock market. The periodic deposits are her earnings, or portions of them. I should add that the time periods are also indicative."

"You mean that they were at six month intervals?" I'd been wondering about that.

"And, more recently, nine months or more. That is because several years ago the tax laws were changed, requiring nine, instead of six months, before a tax advantage occurs to the seller of securities. Naturally, Miss Williams would know that?"

Ron nodded, realized that wasn't enough for my aunt, and said, "Yes."

Aunt Kay sighed. "It's a mistake that parents who don't physically abandon their children make too. That gold can make up for love."

"Why did she wait so long, Aunt Kay? I mean, that woman who was here. She was no kid."

"That idea again that you can make up for not being with your child. She wanted it to be an amount so splendid, so lavish, that her daughter would understand how much she really loved her. The longer she waited, the more money she would have. And like everything else in life, the longer she put it off, the harder it got. I'm sure her original intention was to meet her daughter when she gave her the money; their first face to face confrontation since she gave her up."

"But she didn't meet her."

Ron was getting impatient again. I could tell by the way he interrupted.

"Which is why you're here, isn't it, Mr. Van Cleave? Because something happened to force her hand and make her disappear at the same time."

It sure was, I thought to myself. It's why we're all here. And that was when the phone rang. I remember it exactly because I was looking at Ron with my aunt's words going through my head. And also because Aunt Kay broke one of her rules. She answered the phone herself, something she never did, and after saying hello, listened for a moment and then handed the receiver to Ron.

It was the call from New York. Of course I knew even before Ron turned in my direction and gestured for something to write on, and I leaned across and got him the pad and pen from my aunt's desk.

When he had hung up, he sat back in his chair and told us what had been found out in New York.

"Well," he said, "that was my father's assistant on the phone. I guess these are the . . . uh . . . pertinent facts. First, her name is Susan Kilgore and she lives at 1636 Franklin and her phone number is WEstview 5-8642. He must also have talked to somebody who knows her pretty well because he found out that she'd been married when she was about eighteen but divorced the guy after only three months."

He hesitated and looked closely at his notes. "Oh, yeah, the grounds were mental and physical cruelty. Apparently, he beat on her. There's something about her losing a modeling job because she showed up with a black eye that couldn't be hidden by the make-up."

"Is there anything more about this husband? I mean aside from his being a violent type?"

Aunt Kay seemed rather thoughtful. I wondered if she was thinking along the same lines as I was.

"Not much," he responded. "Vietnam vet. Worked for a while as a part-time stunt man for a couple of the TV series."

"I think," I said, "that we shouldn't waste any time getting to our Ms. Kilgore. Her ex sounds like the kind of dude who could frighten an old schoolteacher pretty good. Don't you think, Aunt Kay?"

But before she could answer, Ron said, "I was just getting to that. My father's assistant said that they told him she was out doing a three-day shoot on a TV commercial they're filming up at Lake Arrowhead. Even if they finish today, it won't be until late and it's unlikely she'd come back before morning."

"In that case," said Aunt Kay, happily accepting the prospect of being able to get to her literary recordings after all, "Mrs. Di has a list of chores she must do around town and for which she needs your assistance. Mr. Van Cleave, why don't you plan to dine with us tonight? Regardless of your father's assistant's opinion on Ms. Kilgore's itinerary for today, I think it would be worth a call to her after dinner, don't you?"

He did.

What he didn't think was worth anything was my suggestion that he join Mrs. Di and I on our excursion around town. I don't know which got me madder at myself, breaking my vow not to give him another chance to reject me like that or not being more persistent in my recipe file search for a palate pleaser made from poisonous toadstools. Believe me, he'd have dined on Deadly Nightshade burgers if I'd had my way.

As it was, we'd barely sat down to the first course of cold beet soup when the doorbell rang. Mrs. Di was busy serving from the tureen so I volunteered, remarking as I passed his chair, "This is the way it all started for us, Ronald dahling, cold soup and you ringing the doorbell. Who knows, maybe I'll get lucky again."

He didn't even bat an eye. I, however, did. The eye with which I peered through the peephole and saw Bruce Downley standing outside my aunt's door.

11.

Aunt Kay wasn't exactly thrilled when I scurried back to inform her, leaving Bruce outside, still ringing.

The doorbell rang once more and there was a long moment of silence — except for Ron's maddeningly hearty slurping of his soup. You would have thought he didn't even care that handsome, successful, worldly, and charming Bruce Downley was standing poised on my threshold. Finally Aunt Kay dealt with it in her own inimitable fashion.

"Do I owe this intrusion to you, Lisa? Have you bewitched this young banker? Is that why he shows up uninvited and unannounced in the middle of my dinner?"

That was Aunt Kay's idea of humor. There isn't much that gets past her and she was obviously aware of the atmosphere which had developed between Ron and myself.

"I'm sure he's here to see you on business," I

said, sneaking a glance at Ron to see if her remarks had struck home.

The doorbell rang again.

"You had better let him in." Aunt Kay sighed. "He can wait in the study until we finish and we'll have our coffee in there with him."

That turned out to be easier said than done. Bruce Downley's idea was that he'd see my aunt immediately. I'd gotten him into the study all right but it didn't look as though I'd be able to persuade him to wait there, when Mrs. Di appeared with a tray of refreshments for him that included soda, brandy, port, and cheese and crackers. It did the trick and I was able to rejoin Aunt Kay and Ron in time to finish the entree.

As soon as we were back in the study, I introduced Bruce Downley to Aunt Kay while Mrs. Di poured the coffee, and he started right in, setting the tone with his opening statement.

"I'd give my next promotion to know how much you already knew when Mr. Gulden brought you into my office."

He softened it with a smile, or tried to, but it wasn't much of a smile. The dazzle was gone. There was plenty of tension showing in the handsome face too. He turned to my aunt.

"Maybe I should re-phrase that, Mrs. Farraday? How much did you already know when you sent them?"

"I think not, Mr. Downley." Aunt Kay was the picture of composure. "I think the relevant question is what do *you* know *now* that has brought you bursting into my home?"

Bruce seemed to think that over while taking his first sip of coffee. He looked back up at Aunt Kay and his expression was still distracted. "I don't think I follow you, Mrs. Farraday?"

"I don't see why not. The trail is clear enough. Earlier, Mr. Gulden called to give me the information you were kind enough to search out. Then I requested even more information and Mr. Gulden agreed, stressing that he would have to apply pressure to overcome your understandable reluctance to further involve yourself in an enterprise which offered you no profit. And now you suddenly show up here, asking insinuating questions. I don't have to see you, sir, to know that you are upset and that what has upset you is what you found out in trying to fill my request for further details on those checks."

"And I say you sent your niece, if she is your niece, and her boyfriend to lull me into — "

"Mr. Van Cleave's relationship is a business one. He is our client." Aunt Kay was at her iciest. "If you can't control your mind well enough to avoid insinuations and assumptions you will leave my house."

Bruce flushed. He took a deep breath and dug the knuckles of both hands into his eyes.

"You're right. It's just that . . . well, what I found out caught me by surprise. I'm sorry and I do apologize."

He removed the knuckles, blinked, and looked slowly at each of us. "You have to understand. . . ." He stopped and shrugged. "On the other hand, why should you? I'll just say that

Mr. Gulden kept his promise about applying pressure."

Aunt Kay waited. "Why don't you tell us what you know?"

He had pulled himself together and it looked like it would stick. "I'm not so sure," he said in an even, controlled voice, the one he'd used in his office but which was now putting in its first appearance, "that I will tell you anything. Not until you have told me a few things, first."

"Mr. Downley, obviously you have had a shock. You found something unexpected and difficult to deal with. You must know — and this is in no way a threat, I don't threaten people — but you must know that if you refuse to enlighten us now, I will inform Mr. Gulden to that effect."

He nodded. "I guess I'm pretty much in between the rock and the hard place."

"I have no ill-feeling toward you, Mr. Downley."

Aunt Kay's tone was softer. I knew that meant she was moving in for the kill.

She went on: "But you can hardly expect me to reveal matters which are constrained by the confidentiality between a lawyer and a client."

"Of course I knew you'd say that." Bruce didn't seem too impressed.

"But most importantly," Aunt Kay concluded, "you couldn't expect me to tell you anything at all until you have revealed whether your information is pertinent to the matter I have undertaken or not."

"Meaning I open up to you, and then once

you've found out what you want to know you'll just tell me that you have nothing pertinent to add, right?" he said bitterly.

"Stop stalling, please, Mr. Downley." Aunt Kay could say the hardest things in the softest voice. "Why not tell us graciously? You must realize that sooner or later Mr. Gulden will be able to trace your footsteps through the bank's records and we will have the information inevitably. Why not keep our gratitude and esteem by saving us that chore? You have everything to gain and nothing to lose."

He chewed that one over for a minute or two. But I could already see the sag going out of his face and knew he must have made his mind up.

To get him started, Aunt Kay gave him a little push.

"Were those checks she deposited over the years from many different brokerage houses or did Miss Williams tend to use the same firms or firm?"

She got her effect. Poor Bruce's mouth dropped open before he could catch himself. When he did, he turned it into a tight little smile, not the dazzler, of course, and said, "You're too clever for me, I guess. Always one jump ahead."

"Not necessarily." Aunt Kay could afford to be modest. "Merely establishing the fact that I cannot be flim-flammed."

Bruce nodded. "Well, you're right, of course, they were from brokerage houses. A lot of different ones. Your Miss Williams must have shopped around," he added.

"All but one? Isn't that what you said, Mrs.

Farraday?" Ron interjected. I imagine he must have been feeling left out and figured it was time to remind everybody he was the originator of it all.

"That's right." Bruce didn't seem like he was holding back anymore. But he kept his eyes on Aunt Kay. "The first check, the one for six thousand dollars, was a personal check, drawn on our bank."

That was it all right, that's what had gotten to him and brought him there to my aunt's. He reached over for the brandy bottle again and poured a drop or two into his cup, not looking up again until he'd added fresh, hot coffee from the pot and stirred it all slowly.

"Does the name Foster Llewelyn mean anything to you?"

Aunt Kay looked thoughtful for a moment and then said, "No. I don't think so."

Both Ron and I knew he didn't expect an answer from either of us and kept quiet. After a swallow of coffee and brandy, Bruce Downley went on.

"I'm not really surprised. Even though he's one of the richer men around. He's always been a loner and now that he's older he has apparently become a recluse."

"Apparently?" Aunt Kay was still keeping the sharpness out of her voice.

"I don't know him personally," Bruce explained with a sarcastic little laugh. "Junior executives at banks aren't usually given to hanging around with the customers who have accounts in the eight figure class."

He finished the coffee and declined politely when I offered to get some more, smiling at me with his eyes, the first time in a while that he'd taken them off Aunt Kay. He may have been haggard and harassed, but Bruce Downley had nice eyes.

"What I know about him I know second-hand." The eyes were back on Aunt Kay. "Of course a certain amount is public knowledge. I don't mind telling you when I found out that check came from him, it shook me up. You don't know anything about him so you wouldn't understand that."

"No. Tell us." Aunt Kay's face was expressionless.

"Well . . ." Bruce looked around, first to me, then to Ron, and back to me. "I want some assurance that what I tell you, what I have told you, is to remain confidential."

"Aren't you a little late in asking that?" Aunt Kay was nice but firm. "You have already divulged the name."

"What I want to know is who else will know? Who will you tell?"

"I can assure you, Mr. Downley, that any information you give us, including the name Foster Llewelyn, will go no further than" — Aunt Kay made a gesture which took in Ron and myself — "my client and immediate family."

"I see." Bruce hesitated, looking very thoughtful.

"Of course," said Aunt Kay, "there is Mr. Gulden. I assume you will tell him as well."

"I think," Bruce Downley said very slowly, "I would rather not."

"No?" Aunt Kay raised her eyebrows.

"No." Bruce turned to me. "Lisa, I believe I will take you up on that offer of more coffee now."

I started toward the kitchen but ran into Mrs. Di in the hall. She said she would get it and I returned to my chair.

"You see," Bruce was saying as I sat, "it's common knowledge around banking circles that this man Foster Llewelyn once expected to acquire the controlling interest in First Industrial and that it was Bert Gulden's vote that blocked the acquisition."

Bruce stopped. Mrs. Di had entered with a fresh pot of coffee, and he waited until she had poured, set the pot down, and left. He did, however, thank us both for the coffee, Mrs. Di in words and me, I might as well admit it, with his eyes.

He shifted back to Aunt Kay and continued. I should mention here something that I had noticed from the first about Aunt Kay. People always talked to her as if she could see, even when they knew she couldn't. It probably had something to do with the alertness in her face. I know I had done it myself right from the first. And so did everyone else. Bruce Downley was no exception. He was looking at her intently as he said, "After that, Foster Llewelyn used every bit of his influence to make sure that Mr. Gulden never became president of First Industrial. So it hardened into a standoff. Both men had their supporters and their feud split First Industrial into two camps. Even though now, so many years later, the original issue no longer exists, the two camps still do. With control of a major bank at stake, there are always plenty of issues. If you know anything about the banking game you know that it's rough. The men who have made it to the top spend a lot of time stepping on the faces of those who are just below them.

"Mrs. Farraday, I owe Bertram Gulden a great deal. He has encouraged and aided my career unstintingly, but I do not want to put myself in the middle if I can help it. Besides, I don't know how well you know Mr. Gulden, but if that fine gentleman has a blind spot anywhere, it's Foster Llewelyn. If there were even the slightest suspicion that I had anything to do with his old archenemy, well, at the very least, it would hurt Mr. Gulden."

"And at the most, Mr. Downley?" Aunt Kay's cross-examination tone suddenly cut sharply into Bruce's explanation. "If your position is that vulnerable, would you prefer to no longer provide the key link in our chain of information?"

"Well, I actually don't see what further purpose I could serve anyway."

"Two come to mind," Aunt Kay answered promptly. "First, if there were any more financial transactions involving Miss Emmaline Williams —"

"Didn't I make myself clear?" His voice had risen. "Old man Llewelyn could bring me nothing but grief. I mean to stay as far away from that vicious old pirate as possible."

Aunt Kay nodded. "I accept that, but I was thinking of transactions of a different nature, not necessarily involving Mr. Llewelyn."

"What nature? There's someone else involved, you mean?"

"I haven't said that. I merely want us to have the opportunity to explore any and all possibilities," Aunt Kay answered smoothly.

Bruce didn't answer at all. I had to look away. I hated to see the poor guy squirm. It was obvious that he was totally shook by what he'd let himself in for. Of course I knew that my aunt was thinking of something to do with the woman we knew now to be Miss Williams' daughter.

And then an incredible thing happened. Bruce Downley's voice broke into my thoughts. "You think I'm really a wimp, don't you, Lisa?"

I turned to find those deep, handsome eyes fixed directly on me. After a moment that seemed like a year, he took them away to face Aunt Kay again and I was glad I hadn't had to answer.

"A lot of people get the wrong idea about me," he said, as much to himself as to us, "that I'm a human computer, all head and no heart. Well, Mr. Gulden put this on a personal basis from the start. Okay, I buy that. Now." He cleared his throat. "You mentioned there were two purposes I could serve. What's the second one?"

"You could give us all the information you have about Foster Llewelyn," Aunt Kay responded blithely.

There was a pause and then he smiled and said ruefully, "You don't like to make it too easy, do you, Mrs. Farraday?"

"Life sees to that, I'm afraid, Mr. Downley."

"All right, in for a penny, in for a pound, as *my* great aunt used to say. First, nobody knows much about him. Not even at the bank, and from what I could gather, it provided a lot of the capital for the empire he built in the old days."

"By 'old days' you mean how long ago?" Aunt Kay was back to cross-examining again.

"Oh, almost a quarter century. He's a throwback, an old maverick who made his fortune in Alaska during the oil pipeline boom time. A real roughneck who came out of nowhere, a loner who still doesn't trust anybody and always operated on sheer gut instinct. He seems to be one of those storybook characters you always hear about and never really find. A self-made man who started from scratch with no connections, no family, no capital, and pulled it off. About fifteen or twenty years ago he settled down here and has managed to get his thumb into a good many profitable pies, although I understand he hasn't been too active lately. Of course nobody ever knows what someone like him, a lone wolf, is up to."

Bruce went on a little longer and I made notes on everything he said, but that was the gist of it. Finally it was obvious that he'd run out of information, and Aunt Kay said we'd better call it a night and thanked him. I saw him to the door.

"I just hope you haven't gotten in over your head, Lisa," was Bruce's parting remark. "Of course I'm in the dark as to exactly where that old shark fits into your investigation. He paused and gave me a long, searching look. "Hey!" he finally said. "Listen to me warning *you*! If this thing blows up, the nicest thing that'll happen to me is I'll lose my job."

But he didn't fool me. There was a twinkle in his eye. He'd finally made a commitment to help somebody, and I knew how good that could feel. Not to mention that when he shook my hand goodbye his was very warm and he did hold mine just a heartbeat longer than necessary.

12.

"I hope the silly smile you've got on your face doesn't mean that you were taken in by that grandstand play."

Ron had sidled casually alongside to lay that zinger on me just as soon as I stepped back inside the study. Aunt Kay was behind her desk and was obviously lost in thought, probably going over what we'd just found out.

"It means," I told him, "that I am glad my Great Aunt Catharine and I still have Mr. Downley's extremely necessary cooperation and assistance in *your* case. As for what your attitude means, I suggest you consult a child psychologist."

"I've seen lots of dudes like him. When I went to acting school. Superficially goodlooking." He shot a glance at me and I smiled back innocently. "They had to be loved, needed the constant attention. He's probably sticking in this because of your friend, Mr. Gulden. This guy Downley is strictly a climber."

"Yes." Aunt Kay was chewing her upper lip. "The figure of Bertram Gulden hovered throughout Mr. Downley's recital. It has occurred to me that Mr. Gulden was very prompt to offer his help. Of course I was predisposed to attribute it to our old friendship."

"Aunt Kay!" I was shocked. "You're not getting suspicious of Mr. Gulden, are you? Really?"

"I am afraid old age is not what it's cracked up to be, my dear. It is generally supposed to bring wisdom. It certainly breeds cynicism. I am suspicious of everyone until proven otherwise.

"Nevertheless, we must face facts and it is a fact that Mr. Gulden is still not president of the First Industrial Bank & Trust Co. Might he not have discovered Miss Williams' existence and in his passion for revenge on an old and implacable foe decided that she was the perfect instrument to wreak that vengeance?"

"Do you mean that Mr. Gulden kidnapped her or something?" Ron sounded like he didn't believe Mr. Gulden was involved any more than I did.

"No, I don't say that. But I don't disregard it, either."

"But what about the daughter, Aunt Kay? Did Mr. Gulden find out about her too? And why would he have agreed to help us if he did?"

Aunt Kay scowled. "Well, what shall we do next?"

I jumped on that. "Let's go to this — Susan Kilgore you said her name is, Ron? And tell her we've found out who her real father is and she'll have to show us that 'Niobe' letter. Of course that would make what you told Bruce a lie, that you would only reveal the information he gave us to your client and your immediate family, but what the heck."

"My 'confidential assistant' has learned a little something, at least. But a little learning is a dangerous thing. First, it would hardly make my statement a lie since I did not stipulate *whose* immediate family, and Ms. Kilgore is certainly the immediate family of Miss Williams and very probably of Mr. Foster Llewelyn. Secondly, the right, indeed the duty, to lie in the service of a client is as old as the legal profession itself.

"Last, and most important," she was going on, "let's not make things more complicated than they are. Finding Miss Williams is our objective; the letter and the daughter are secondary now. Obviously, unless the wool has been pulled completely over our eyes, she is not with her daughter. But, going on our supposition that she felt she was in danger, might not Miss Williams have sought the protection of someone who had the power of wealth? Or, if that same power were the source of the danger she felt, it is not impossible that she would have gone to face it head on."

Aunt Kay made that gesture of hers, extending a hand and turning the palm over.

"In either event, we are also not positive yet that Foster Llewelyn *is* the father of Miss Williams' daughter. I must see him. And since I cannot, and since you, Lisa, are my eyes, I would like you and Mr. Van Cleave to go to Mr.

Llewelyn's home tomorrow and talk to him about the situation."

"Sure." I admit that Bruce Downley had made him sound scary, but he had also made him sound interesting. "You know where he lives?"

"I will by tomorrow. Mr. Van Cleave, have you anything you would like to add or ask?"

"Uh . . . I'm not sure. . . ."

Ron was distracted, looking around as if he was missing something. He turned toward me.

"Lisa, did you see where I put that piece of paper on which I wrote down the information from New York about Susan Kilgore?"

"Sure. You put it down when we went into the dining room to eat."

"But where? I don't see it on the table."

"I think you left it on your chair."

"I'm sure I left it on the table."

"Stand up, you're probably sitting on it."

"I'm positive I left it on the table."

But he got up. And he was right, it wasn't on the chair. It was on the floor under the chair and had been obscured by their legs — his and the chair's — until he stood up. I saw it right away and told him so, and he picked it up.

"Mr. Van Cleave, we can expect you in the morning then?"

Aunt Kay got up too. Obviously she was thinking of calling it a night.

"Mrs. Farraday?" Ron had turned toward her. "I did just remember something. Didn't Downley mention something about this Foster Llewelyn making his money in Alaska?"

"On the oil pipeline." Aunt Kay had, of course, picked up on the excitement in Ron's voice even though she hadn't the advantage I had of also seeing it in his face.

"One time at Miss Williams' I remember I was telling her how the thing I missed most about being away from home was the change of seasons, especially Christmas with snow. And she said that if I'd lived in Alaska like she had, I'd feel just like she did, only too happy never to see snow again."

"Excellent." Aunt Kay was almost beaming, or as close as she'll ever get to a beam. "The dates fit and now the place. All the more reason for you to see Foster Llewelyn tomorrow. Good night."

Ron went out of the room ahead of me, Aunt Kay calling out a reminder for me to tell Mrs. Di to set another place for breakfast in the morning.

"Y'know," Ron protested as we walked down the hall, "you don't really have to feed me every time I show up."

"Don't be silly, dahling. I have been searching out some wonderful new recipes just for you. A unique mushroom omelette," I told him while showing him to the door and closing it gently but swiftly before he had a chance to offer a hand. One handsome man shaking my hand each night is all that I can handle.

13.

The first thought that popped into my head when Ron had nosed his old Maverick up over the last of the rolling hills crowning the posh suburb of Bel-Air and into an area of even more massive traditional houses was that the people who lived there had no idea of such trifles as energy crisis or recessions. We drove in between stone gateposts. The huge iron gates had a certain majesty about them, reminding me of the castles and drawbridges in fairy tales. The lawn stretched like a meadow in an old English poem. Its grass was a dark, patchy green.

The drive curved around toward the side of a mansion. That was the only word to describe it. I could see tennis courts beyond, tufts of grass sprouting up from the cracked, unused clay. Ron parked to one side of a car port under which stood a Chrysler with M.D. plates.

We had barely gotten out of the car before the man appeared. He had on the kind of white jacket that servants wear, but there was no mistaking the flat cheekbones set high in a bronzed face underneath the watchful eyes. Later, when I remembered about Alaska, it occurred to me that he was probably Eskimo, but in the split second when he popped up in front of me without having made a sound, I didn't have time to think.

"Would you tell Mr. Llewelyn that Mr. Van Cleave and Ms. Farraday would like to see him," I heard Ron's voice say.

"He don't see anybody. Sorry." He barely moved his lips and his voice was soft and hard at the same time.

"Would you tell him that it's about his wife?"

"Doctor's here." He shook his head. "He don't have a wife, anyways."

"He did. Tell him that it's about Emmaline Williams." Ron was persistent, I had to give him points for that.

"Is she here now?" I figured it was worth a shot. But there was no catching him off guard. His eyes never so much as flickered in my direction. "Wait here." He turned and was gone.

"Some place, isn't it?" I commented after a while.

"I don't like it." Ron had begun to pace in a semi-circle alongside the car. "It gives me the creeps."

"I know. It's awesome and it reeks of money, but it's also so cold and empty of life. As if it was really abandoned and we all just happened to show up here at the same time, like characters in a play."

"Maybe we've just got abandonment on our

minds," Ron mumbled back and we both fell silent.

A couple of minutes later the man appeared again from nowhere and motioned for us to follow him. I thought he would be taking us inside, but to my surprise he led us over to some wicker furniture set around a table and umbrella near a cluster of banana palms.

"Wait," he mumbled and disappeared again.

It wasn't long before a door opened and a little bald-headed man, what my father would term a "squirt," emerged carrying a black bag and with a nurse in uniform bringing up the rear. He trotted straight for the Chrysler, but it was the nurse, who was fully a head taller, who got behind the wheel. I was occupying my mind with aimless speculation over that little scene when I became aware of movement out of the corner of my eye.

I focused and agreed with my first impression that "movement" was the proper word to describe it. "Walking" certainly wasn't.

The man with the steel-grey hair was tall and excruciatingly thin and he leaned, between lurches forward, on the shoulder and arm of the Eskimo. From what we had found out about him I had estimated that Foster Llewelyn couldn't be more than sixty-eight years old, but moving like that he looked more like one hundred and sixty-eight. As soon as he got close, of course, I could see I was wrong. One look in his eyes and you knew he was a thousand and sixty-eight.

"We're sorry to put you to this trouble," Ron

began, standing politely. "We could have come inside. We didn't know you weren't well."

"Damn your impudence." The cold, dead-grey eyes flashed. "Who asked for your sympathy?"

The Eskimo lowered him into a chair.

"All right, Man," he rasped. "I'll call."

The Eskimo padded off and the mean old eyes raked us both.

"For that matter, who asked for you at all?"

"We hoped that you might know the whereabouts of your wife, Mr. Llewelyn."

"You're not only impudent, you're a presumptuous jackass. I have no wife."

Ron was unperturbed. "Or that you would like to know about your daughter?"

"I thought at first you were merely a lying young punk. But you're dangerous. You have a death wish." Purple-veined eyelids closed over those terrible eyes.

"Please," he said, managing to make "please" sound arrogant, "take your girl and go have that wish fulfilled elsewhere."

"We know about the check you gave Emmaline Williams." Ron was hanging in there. "Six thousand dollars. That was the year your daughter turned six, Mr. Llewelyn. One thousand dollars for every year of her life. Of course, you probably weren't so rich nineteen years ago."

The eyes opened and for the first time seemed to really look at us, to try to see us. Then the hard glaze formed over them again and the voice rasped out.

"Any record of a check of mine would be in the microfilm files of the First Industrial Bank

& Trust Co. Who put you up to this? Who'd dare send a couple of young kids like you?"

"It's not something we have to be 'put up to.' We're trying to find Miss Williams. We're worried that something may have happened to her. She was tutoring me in economics and —"

"It must have been Perkins or McVay." The rasp was even uglier, if possible. "Gulden would love to see me squirm, but he's always been too respectable." He made "respectable" sound like a dirty word.

I couldn't help myself. "Mr. Llewelyn, please." It wasn't that I thought he might respond more readily to a woman's approach. He'd already made his attitude toward me perfectly clear. It was simply that I couldn't just sit there like a dummy any longer. "We only want to know if Miss Williams is all right. If she's here, please put our minds at ease. If she's not, do you know where she is? Has she been in touch with you?"

The lids had come down again and he didn't answer. This time when they came up it was like a curtain rising on an empty stage. When he finally spoke, his voice was as flat and empty as his eyes.

"I know nothing," he said, "of any Emmaline Williams. If there is such a person and she endorsed any one of the literally thousands of checks I have written in the course of my extensive business dealings, I no longer recall how or why and I don't care."

But Ron wasn't letting go. "That just won't go down anymore, Mr. Llewelyn. And you do have a daughter, too, whether you know it or not.

Whether you want to believe it or not. And, if Miss Williams is hurt in any way, I don't care how much money you —"

"Man!"

It was meant to be a shout, but it came out more like a loud gasp. For somebody who didn't make any sounds, the Eskimo was certainly good at hearing them. He was there in a couple of seconds, one powerful arm stretched out for Foster Llewelyn to take, the other hanging easily at his side like a club. The old man, breathing heavily, his face completely drained of color, hoisted himself up against the powerful shoulder and they began the same awkward, lurching shuffle back toward the house.

The Eskimo never looked at us. Not even when he said, "Don't be here when I come back. You make him sick."

The feeling was mutual.

14.

I tried to think of myself as a videotape machine. Sitting there in Aunt Kay's study, I wanted to give her as complete and accurate a picture of our meeting with Foster Llcwelyn as if she had been present herself. After I was through and had mentally clicked the playback switch in my head to "off," Aunt Kay thanked me and asked for our conclusions or impressions, if any.

Ron had been sitting beside me, making little additions or corrections throughout, and he started off by admitting that my aunt and I had been right.

"If not," he said, "if there hadn't been a strong connection between him and Miss Williams, a mean old buzzard like that would just have ordered us thrown out. That he had to come hobbling out of his lair is proof that it was important for him to get a look at us and find out what we were up to. Any odds you care to name . . . that he was Miss Williams' husband. And probably the father of her daughter."

111

"Were you both completely satisfied that Miss Williams wasn't there?"

"No."

"No."

That was a first. Flabbergasted at agreeing on something for once, we both turned and stared at each other.

Ron recovered first.

"Don't forget," he pointed out, "we were never let inside the house. And even though that attack he had at the end looked real enough, gasping for air and all, how do we know it wasn't a fake?"

Aunt Kay asked if there was anything else we remembered that might indicate Miss Williams' presence. After a moment's reflection we both had to admit that there wasn't.

"Then neither of you is convinced that she was there; it is merely a possibility which you don't want to rule out. Is it any more likely that Mr. Llewelyn merely knows where she has fled? That he is in touch with her?"

We shook our heads in unison.

Aunt Kay sighed. "Perhaps if we had not been so direct, you might have found out for sure."

"I don't know," said Ron, doubtfully. "He'd be pretty hard to fool into revealing anything if he didn't want to."

"True." Aunt Kay nodded. "As you describe him, he is hardly the man a woman would turn to anyway. Especially once she had turned away."

Aunt Kay got up and walked over to the globe of the world and gave it a couple of whirls before she continued.

112

"From your account, Lisa, his actions certainly gave him away. Especially when you told him about his daughter. It doesn't sound as though he knew she existed?"

Ron and I nodded in agreement.

"You described him as tall and thin, the same basic structure as Susan Kilgore." She nodded in satisfaction. "Everything," she said, "especially the style of his denial, serves to confirm our theory, all right."

Aunt Kay got back behind her desk.

"Get Susan Kilgore's number and dial it for me, Lisa, please. We don't want to let up now."

I got the sheet of paper with the information about Susan Kilgore from Ron and did as I had been asked. As soon as it started ringing, I handed the receiver to Aunt Kay.

"I may have to do some pretty fancy coercing to get her up here right away," she said, her hand cupped over the mouthpiece. "But, as I said, it's important not to let up."

If by "get her up here right away" my aunt meant that day, I found myself thinking a little later, she could forget it. That was after we had tried her number several times and, as a last resort, even put in a call to the advertising agency she had been doing the commercial up at Lake Arrowhead for. Her number, of course, hadn't answered, and the best the agency could do for us, after verifying that the commercial had finished shooting on schedule, was to supply the number of the service she used to take messages for her when she wasn't at home. That, Ron informed me, was a very common thing for actors and models, especially if they lived alone, as we had been informed was the case with Susan Kilgore.

That was a pretty rough evening. After a few more futile attempts at her home number, Aunt Kay had called the service and left a message for Susan to call her. That only made it worse because then we were not only marking time between attempts to reach her, we were also waiting for the phone to ring in case she had called her service and picked up our message.

When Mrs. Di had come in to inquire what she should do about dinner, Aunt Kay told her she had no appetite herself and the issue was passed to Ron and me. He got up and said he was going home and we could reach him there if anything happened. It will give you some idea of the state of my morale when I tell you that I didn't even try to devise some scheme for getting him to reconsider and spend some time with me.

The next morning I had about decided that my stomach could do without breakfast just as well as it had done without dinner, when Aunt Kay appeared and asked me what I was doing.

"Getting my bathing suit," I told her. "I haven't been down to the pool since this whole thing began. I don't want to face the fact that the only reason I spent any time there before was because of him. Logic, at least my kind of logic, demands that I spend some time there now that he's definitely not going to be in view."

"That is no kind of logic."

"A reason, then. I'm not going back to Saratoga Springs after having spent a summer in glorious, sunny California with a chalkier body than I left with. Besides, who knows? Maybe I'll meet an even cuter lifeguard who will have an even bigger problem he'd like to share."

Aunt Kay showed her teeth. She, of course, thinks that she's smiling when she does that. "I suggest instead that you call as soon as possible on Ms. Susan Kilgore at her place of residence."

"You spoke to her?"

"No. I'm tired of waiting. I expect you to stir something up. If you will come with me to the study and phone Mr. Van Cleave to drive over, I will outline how I think you should approach her."

"All right," I said, and tossed the bathing suit back in the drawer.

It turned out that Susan Kilgore didn't live very far away. Her address was a complex of apartments, two stories high, on Franklin, not far from downtown Hollywood. We walked through the courtyard which was formed and enclosed by the apartments themselves.

It took about five frustrating minutes of ringing and knocking before Ron turned to me and asked if I had any bright ideas, because otherwise he felt like breaking the door down and ransacking her apartment for the letter if she truly wasn't inside.

"And maybe even if she is," he added bitterly.

Poor Ron. The pressure was really getting to him. I couldn't blame him for feeling disgusted. After the breakthrough on finding out the identity of Miss Williams' daughter and then Bruce Downley's coming up with the husband and probable father for us, it looked as though we had it made. Except suddenly everything had come to a standstill.

"Maybe I do have a bright idea," I told him. "Let's go back to the car and I'll tell you about it."

He had some objections at first, probably because I had thought of it instead of him.

"After all, you thought I could pass for *your* kid sister," I reminded him as we drove back to the Chateau Marmont.

My Great Aunt Catharine, however, would be a different story as I darn well knew. Ron had done his basic rationalization bit, warned me to be careful and not take unnecessary risks, and naturally wound up emphasizing that he'd be standing by to take over in case I messed up. Aunt Kay wouldn't waste any breath on warnings or rationalizations. She'd just flat out veto it. The way around that was not telling her what I was going to do. Which meant sneaking into the apartment, getting the props I needed to pull off my brainstorm, and sneaking out again without her knowing I had been there. I got lucky. Letting myself in with my key, I heard clanging pans and rising voices from the kitchen. My aunt and Mrs. Di were at it again. One of their culinary confrontations.

It wasn't until we were back in the parking lot of Susan Kilgore's apartment and Ron was backing into a spot that he said what I'd been expecting him to say all along.

116

"Y'know, I'm surprised your aunt went along with your idea. I mean, it is kind of against the law, isn't it?"

"Only technically. You ought to realize by now that my aunt has the fullest confidence in me. We both know how to bend the law without breaking it. It's an art," I added, to really put him in his place. "Better give me fifteen minutes before calling," I told him and climbed out.

First I went back up and banged on Susan Kilgore's door a few more times, alternating it with pushing her bell. Satisfied that she hadn't come in while we were gone, I walked around until I found the superintendent's apartment.

When S. Wagner (the name printed above the bell) opened his door to my ring, he turned out to be a long, lanky man with large brown eyes and a slow, lazy kind of smile.

"Sorry miss, but we don't have any vacancies right now," he said, looking at the two suitcases I held, one in each hand. "If you'd like to fill out an application?"

"I'm not looking for an apartment, I'm looking for my sister. My stepsister, Susie. Susan Kilgore?"

He put the sheet of paper he'd gotten back on a table inside the door.

"Miss Kilgore? She's number twenty-eight. You make a left and at the end turn right and at the first stairs —"

"I know," I told him nicely. "I was just there but she doesn't answer. I came on an earlier flight than she originally expected and I couldn't phone her because she was up shooting this television commercial in Arrowhead Lake. Did

you know my big sister is a television model?"
I tried to make it as gushy as I could. And to
keep talking as fast as I could because I didn't
want to give him too much time to think anything over.

"Could you please open her apartment for me
so I could wait for Susie inside? I know she
won't be long, but — "

S. Wagner had turned out, for all his soft,
lazy brown eyes and slow smile, to be a pretty
suspicious dude. He was really looking me over.
I had already mentally patted myself on the
back for calling myself her stepsister to cover
any lack of resemblance, as well as for grabbing
the two most humungous suitcases I could find,
figuring it would take a pretty rotten creep to
force a young girl to lug those all over. So he
was already wavering when I finished up with
my last stroke.

"I've just got to have someplace to freshen
up. You see, I got sick on the plane. It was my
first time ever. Flying, I mean."

Even before I'd finished, S. Wagner was digging a big ring of keys from one of the pockets
in the mechanic's overall outfit he was wearing.

"C'mon, then," he said, taking one of the suitcases from me and leading the way back to
Susan Kilgore's apartment. Silently I congratu-
lated myself on throwing some clothes and junk
into the suitcases to give them a little real weight
while out loud I said, "Thank you, Stanley."
Which was the name sewn above his breast
pocket.

Naturally he had to go through the routine of

118

ringing and knocking too. I rested my folded arms on the railing of the stairs that led up to her door and looked out over the complex of apartments. I saw Ron's car pull out. He'd wait until he saw me actually enter and then he'd hunt up a pay phone and call according to the plan we'd made. There were kids splashing and playing in a wading pool nestled in the center of the courtyard below.

"Here ya' go, miss."

I turned and saw that Stanley had the door open for me. He swung one suitcase in and I followed, dragging the other. Of course there was that one fleeting moment of half-panic as I stepped inside; that she was actually there all along and just not answering the door or phone. But there was no one in sight as Stanley shut the door behind me, asking me to remind my sister about the perfume samples she was going to get for his wife.

I looked around. Susan Kilgore must have been doing very well. There was a large, sunken living room, a dining area, a kitchen and breakfast nook, and a closed door which I supposed led to the bedroom. It was, I thought, tastefully decorated too. I opened up one of the suitcases and took out a pair of the rubber gloves which Mrs. Di uses for certain cleaning chores and which I had borrowed to use for keeping my fingerprints to myself while I searched Susan Kilgore's apartment for the letter that was signed "Niobe."

That was my complete brainstorm: get myself admitted to the apartment with luggage and a story about being her kid sister and find that letter while Ron kept a look out downstairs. The gloves had been an afterthought — fingerprints always seem to be important to detectives on television — but about a minute after Stanley Wagner had shut the door, I was very glad I'd thought of them. That is, if I was glad about anything at all that had to do with that supposed brainstorm.

The logical thing to do in starting, it seemed to me, was to check out the closed door and verify that it was her bedroom and that Susan wasn't in there, either. Only I couldn't get the door to open more than about eight inches. It kept hitting something and I couldn't budge it. Until finally I pushed with all my might and wedged it open far enough to slide in.

And then I was sorry that I had. Sorry and scared and sick, all at once. The something that the door had kept hitting and sticking against used to be Susan Kilgore. It wasn't her anymore, though. It wasn't anything. Just a body lying with its feet toward the door, one leg straight out and one bent.

15.

It was the phone ringing that snapped me out of it. I guess I can't say I actually fainted, because I never left my feet. When I did come out of whatever it was that I'd faded into, I was leaning forward with my face against the door and both hands flattened against it too. That's why I said I was glad about the rubber gloves. I wouldn't have to worry about my fingerprints being at the scene of a murder.

Don't think I was being overly dramatic or jumping to conclusions. Just before everything in my head had started to whirl around to match the contents of my stomach, I'd seen the heavy looking hunk of metal sculpture lying on the floor. I wasn't going to touch it but I'd've bet that the dried red stuff on it wasn't one of the cosmetics Susan Kilgore used to model.

There was a phone next to the bed but I wasn't going any further into that bedroom than I'd already been. I sort of staggered dizzily into the living room and over to a table where there was another extension and picked it up. I waited, holding it to my ear. Ron's voice, very excited, came after a couple of seconds.

"Lisa?"

"Yes."

"What took you so long? Do you need help or should I keep watch out here?"

"Yes. I mean come up." The connection went and I put the receiver back.

I didn't know if that was the right thing or not. It was bad enough being at the scene of a murder myself without getting Ron involved too. I'm not sure I had even consciously thought it out when I told him to come up, but the fact of the matter was that, murder or no murder, body or no body, I wasn't going to waste the opportunity to look for that letter. It might have been — I can't say for sure even now — that I instinctively felt that the murder, the letter, Ron's missing teacher, the whole thing was somehow connected.

I don't know if my determination to find the letter, even with poor Susan Kilgore lying lifeless a few yards away, sounds cold-blooded to you. It must have to Ron, because he really blew his cool, telling me I was out of my head and he was calling the police immediately to report a crime of violence and what was wrong with me that I thought I could, etc., etc.

But I'm getting ahead of myself. The first thing I did after hanging up the phone was to try to think what Aunt Kay would want me to do. No, that's not exactly correct. I knew she wouldn't want me to be there in the first place. So I reworded my question to myself. What would she need? What would she want me to bring back to her, like that time we went to Miss Williams' house? Of course, the letter, but if I couldn't find that, what else? What else now that Susan Kilgore was dead and I couldn't bring her?

I looked around the room. There was a small desk with two drawers against one wall and I walked over to it. The top drawer was locked, but the key was sticking in the lock and I turned it and slid the drawer open. It held an assortment of notepaper and envelopes and that was all. The second drawer contained stubs of bills, I guess paid ones, some pencils and pens, and a bunch of snapshots with a rubber band around them.

They were all of Susan and the same man. He was goodlooking in a sort of wild, roughneck-looking way. A couple of them showed he and Susan in bathing suits and you could see he liked flexing his muscular body for the camera. The snapshots were all inscribed on the back and all practically the same: "My husband and I on Catalina Island; My husband and I in Acapulco; My husband and I at Big Sur; and so on. Susan Kilgore may have divorced him after a few months, and he may have beat her, but there was no doubt that he still meant something to her, I thought to myself. I had just finished with the last one when there was a soft knock at the door. I put the band back around the snaps and dropped them into the drawer, making sure to shut it. Walking to the door, I called out in what I hoped was a natural voice.

"Who is it?"

And got Ron's voice in response. "Me. Open up."

I don't think there would ever be a time when I wouldn't be glad to see Ron, but never more than right then. Being alone in there was giving me the creeps. Mostly because of the object in the bedroom that meant I wasn't really alone.

He came in swiftly, shutting the door behind him in one motion.

"Wow," he said, looking around admiringly. "Modeling must really pay off. Are those paintings on the walls originals?"

And then I guess he must have noticed something in my face.

"What's the matter? You look like you've seen a —"

"Don't say it," I said and took a step toward him.

He met me halfway and I felt his hands on my shoulders, forcing me to look up at him.

"What's wrong? What's happened?"

It's crazy the way the human mind works, it really is. Despite everything else, I was very much aware that that was the first time Ron had ever held me. I motioned toward the bedroom with my head.

"In there."

He didn't waste any time getting to the bedroom and a moment later I heard him swear under his breath. I knew what he must be going through, I knew what I'd gone through only a few minutes before, but I told myself I had to be strong. I got the other pair of rubber gloves from

124

my suitcase and when Ron walked, white-faced, back into the living room, I handed them to him.

He stared. First at the gloves in my hand, then at the ones I had on, then at me.

"So that we don't leave fingerprints," I explained. "We've got to find that letter," I went on, trying to make it sound as reasonable as it seemed to me.

That was when he blew his cool. When he got to the part about what was wrong with me, "that I thought I could, etc.," I interrupted to tell him that of course we would notify the police, but didn't he think it might be a good idea if he conferred with his attorney first.

That stopped him, but only for a second.

"There's the phone," he said, pointing. "Call her first and then we'll call the police."

That took some thought as to how to handle it. "Obviously you agree with me that she was murdered," I began.

He nodded. "Are you sure it's her? Don't forget, I never saw her."

"It's her," I said. "It seems to me I've heard that the police can get a record from the phone company of any calls made from a particular phone. Which would both involve Aunt Kay and place us here," I went on rapidly. "You see, I was thinking we wouldn't call the police until we left here. It would be better if we asked Aunt Kay about all these things. I mean do you want to tell the police about Miss Williams now?"

"Why not?"

"I don't know, but Aunt Kay will." I could see I had started him having some second thoughts.

"Are you saying the police might suspect Miss Williams?"

"She is her mother, Ron, and she has disappeared. I've always heard that the police suspect the immediate family first in a murder investigation. Anyway, I think that's one of the things we all have to discuss."

"If we split now, what about the Super? He saw you."

"But he didn't see you. And you haven't touched anything, have you?"

"No, but that Super will —"

"Say that he let Susan Kilgore's stepsister into her apartment and give a description that will fit about ten thousand girls in Los Angeles."

"You're crazy, you know that? Rubber gloves!" He snorted. "Where are *your* fingerprints on file? With the FBI?"

"I just felt it was best to be prepared," I answered with dignity. "Look," I said. "I don't suspect Miss Williams and neither do you, but that doesn't mean this isn't tied in some way to her disappearance."

"There's no proof of that."

"If it isn't, it's quite a coincidence. And if I am right, that letter could be an important clue."

"Sure. For the police." Boys can be maddeningly pigheaded. "Why not let the experts do their thing?"

"That won't help Miss Williams. Don't you still care about finding her?"

"You know I do. More than anything. But what about that poor woman lying in there?" He gestured angrily. "She had a discussion with you and your Aunt Kay and it didn't help her much that I can see."

I took a deep breath. That was really a low blow, but I knew it was no time to lose my temper. "The police won't be looking for that letter. They don't even know it exists. If I'm right, finding that letter could do more to get Susan Kilgore's murderer than calling the police an hour or so earlier than we probably will anyway. That's all I'm saying."

I could tell he was wavering and I thought I knew how to convince him. "This could mean Miss Williams is in real danger, Ron. It's more important than ever to locate her."

"It could take hours trying to find that letter," he said doubtfully. "That would be pretty risky, staying here that long."

He looked around the apartment. I had to agree with him there. That apartment was looking bigger and bigger.

"Well, I've already checked out the drawers in this desk. The only thing was some polaroids of Susan and her ex-husband."

He was looking at me. "Lisa," he said, "you and I both know that the most likely place for that letter to be is in her bedroom, don't we? Do you want to search it? Because I don't. Not with her in there."

I didn't say anything. I didn't have to. I'm sure my face said it for me.

"You see?" He reached a hand out for the desk chair, thought better of touching it, and pulled it toward him with his foot instead. He sat and said, "Well, what's your next bright idea?"

I ignored the sarcasm. In fact, I hardly heard it. Because pulling the chair out had dislodged a sweater and jacket that had been draped over its back and across the top of the desk, revealing a little portable typewriter. And the sheet of paper sticking up from it. Ron's eyes had followed mine and he jumped up. But I got to it first.

"Don't touch it," I cried, turning the roller with my gloved hand so all the typing showed clearly.

It was a letter. Not the one we were after, but one Susan Kilgore must've been writing herself.

Dear Chris:

"Sorry to have been slow in answering, but you know I've always been terrible at writing letters. I hope things are still happening for you. It really knocked me out to hear about your job. It sounds really fantastic.

As for me, it's been pretty much the same old story. I just finished a shoot up at Lake Arrowhead. The usual. Nothing interesting to report.

As for my love life, I haven't seen "You Know Who" for over a month, so I guess that's dead. Along those lines, my "Ex" has been around lately, calling and trying to patch things up. He seems to really mean it this time, but I'm very unsure about any reconciliation with him. You know how violent he was when we finally broke up. He says he's a different man now, but I have my doubts. Can you blame me? To tell you the truth, I still see the same rage in his eyes whenever I try to discuss our relationship rationally. I'm afraid that he'll always be hung up on his "macho" image.

But, sucker that I am, I agreed to let him come over tonight to plead his case. Maybe this time I'll finally convince him to get off *my* case. I can imagine you sitting there reading this and shaking your head. Don't worry, if he tries any rough stuff I can always yell for the police. It's just that I feel it's time for me to be adult about it and resolve it with him once and for all. For once he's going to have to listen to me and face reality. There's the doorbell now, so I'll have to finish this after he's gone.

That was all. There was no last name or address of the person she was writing to. I rolled the paper back to its original position.

"It's on the same notepaper that I saw in the top drawer," I said. "And 'Chris' could be the name of either a man or a woman."

"Yeah," Ron said. "Don't tell me you're going to leave it behind for the police? Just because it blows your little theory apart?"

"Sarcasm isn't your best weapon, Ron," I told him. It was something I'd heard my aunt say once.

"I'm too disgusted to be sarcastic," he said. "Let's go."

Unfortunately, I didn't have any weapons left, sarcastic or otherwise. He already had hold of one of my suitcases, and I put the rubber gloves back in the other one, closed it, and followed him to the door. It was either leave or search the bedroom and I knew I wasn't up for that. And never would be. I could hear Ron saying that he'd found a back entrance and we could probably leave that way without being seen, but I was hardly paying any attention. I had turned for one last look at the apartment and all I could think of was, "If I were Susan Kilgore where would I keep a letter from the mother I'd never seen? A letter that gave me one hundred forty three thousand dollars?" Maybe we were wrong about the bedroom? Maybe she would think that was too obvious? Aunt Kay seemed to think that Susan Kilgore was a pretty tricky number. . . .

"Hey, maybe you should've brought a camera. Then you could take a picture, and you wouldn't have to 'memorize' the place."

I turned. Ron had the door open a crack and was peering out.

"What did you say?"

"Huh? What now?" He was staring at me. "C'mon, will you —"

He grabbed for my arm but I shook him off. "Maybe . . . just maybe . . . you've done it again!"

He shut the door. "I've had enough of —" he began but stopped because I wasn't listening. I was heading for one of the paintings on the wall.

" 'Picture,' you said. And before, when you came in, you asked if these paintings were originals. Well, I don't know if this is a reproduction or an original," I said going up to the biggest one and getting my rubber gloves out of the suitcase. "Probably it's a reproduction, but that doesn't matter. If this works I'll never make fun of my mother and the Ladies Fine Arts League of Saratoga Springs again."

I had the gloves on and took the painting off the wall and turned it over. And there it was — a rectangular bulge under the back of the canvas, a sliver of paper showing about a sixteenth of an inch where it had been glued back. I went to the kitchen and got a knife. As I did the delicate job of getting it loose without too much of a mess, Ron found his tongue and asked me how. Actually, he said, "How in the hell — ."

I pulled it all out before answering. One look and there was no doubt. "The artist," I explained, putting the painting back. "Robert *Mother*well."

I left him standing there and returned the knife.

Back in the living room he was still shaking his head.

"It was easy," I said modestly. "I just thought to myself, if I were Susan Kilgore and I had something valuable from a mother I'd never seen, suddenly telling me she was alive and *well* —

"Stop!" he commanded. "I don't want to hear any more. You *are* some kind of Southern California Crazy."

But that time as we headed for the door he carried *both* of my suitcases.

16.

My aunt's reaction, however, was somewhat less enthusiastic.

"I don't understand why you even bothered to bring it, Lisa. Surely it must be obvious that this latest development ends our interest and involvement in the matter of Miss Williams. Of course there will be no bill for you, Mr. Van Cleave, since we are withdrawing without satisfying your commission."

There was a lot more — mostly how the letter (about the husband) in the typewriter showed the murder wasn't connected with our case and how I'd put her in the position of withholding evidence by bringing the "Niobe" letter and she'd have to figure out some way of getting it to the police without having her grandniece's name involved in a murder investigation and so on. I'm just giving you the part I remember best. I don't know if you'll believe me or not, but her deciding to give up like that hurt me a lot more than the bawling out she gave me for my "step-sister" stunt.

I just sat there and took it. Which, as you are probably aware by now, isn't like me. Actually I was totally engrossed in going over the "Niobe" letter in my mind.

Dear Daughter:

Excuse me, but I cannot call you by the name someone else gave you.

First, a word of explanation about the money. Six thousand dollars of it came from your father. Not that he intended it for you. He is not aware of your existence. I was startled to see him by accident, and when, to ease his conscience, he offered me money, I finally accepted a token amount because it was easier than a prolonged argument.

When I had recovered from the shock of hearing about his financial success I realized I could never use any money that came from him. Until it occurred to me that it would be ironic if money from the man who had once denied and ridiculed the practicality of my financial knowledge and theories should be used to prove them. It was only by combining the irony with a rationalization that the money I made would eventually redeem your affection, that I was able to overcome these obstacles and embark on my adventure. You have the proof that my efforts, at least in the material sense, were not in vain.

I have no way of knowing your character, but if such things are hereditary, it is likely that promiscuity is as distasteful to you as it is to me. Therefore, I want you to know that you were not illegitimate. However, marriage to your father was such a devastating error for me that once I came to my senses I had the marriage dissolved, which was possible in Alaska, and resumed my maiden name.

I never stopped dreaming that I would someday appear, wonderfully, magically, in your life and make up for what I had done. But the years went by and even though the money increased, I was never able to bring myself to face you.

Now I know I must never see you. I only hope that the money will provide some small compensation for those more important things which I was not equipped to give you. I wish we could have known each other. Now there is no point in even bothering you with my name.

Goodbye,
Niobe

P.S. Obviously I found and kept track of you. Please don't attempt to reciprocate. It wouldn't be wise and you couldn't find Niobe anyway. She has heeded the call of her father.

That was it. Handwritten on a sheet of plain white paper with only the "Niobe" and the "P.S." handwritten in a different ink. I was just beginning to wonder if there was anything significant about that when Ron's voice broke into my thoughts.

"I still don't understand why you can't keep trying to find Miss Williams?"

Naturally our former client was not exactly thrilled by Aunt Kay's decision to cop out. Aunt Kay wasn't exactly thrilled herself. At least to judge by the tone she took.

"The duly constituted authorities will soon take over that chore, Mr. Van Cleave. It would be presumptuous to think we could compete with the army of trained investigators they will put in the field as soon as they learn of the safety deposit box. They'll want to talk to 'Niobe,' mark my words."

"You're sure they will learn of the safety deposit box?"

"Certainly. Through the keys to it, if nothing else. And, quite naturally, as soon as I have devised a strategem for sending them that infernal letter so that it cannot be traced back to me, I shall do so. Also, remember that the police will have access to Susan Kilgore's adoption records. No, have no fear, sooner or later they will track down your Miss Williams."

"I suppose you're right," he admitted grudgingly. I was saying nothing. "Well, Lisa?" He turned to me. "I guess that's that. We never did go for that pizza. How about right now? A farewell dinner? If that's all right with you, Mrs. Farraday?"

"It's your stomach and intestines."

I got up and Ron stood aside to let me by.

The two of us were almost out of the study when Aunt Kay's voice came.

"Just to satisfy my insatiable curiosity about my fellow human beings — you are both positive that Ms. Kilgore made no mention of her sudden stroke of fortune or reference to her mother in that letter she was typing?"

We answered, "No," and Ron, grasping at the only straw left, asked, "Why? Could that mean something?"

"Probably not." Aunt Kay was emphatic. "You two go enjoy yourselves. I'll have Mrs. DiPasquale inform the police about Susan Kilgore. Anonymously, from a pay phone."

Needless to say, the fact that it was both my first and last date with Ron made that pizza gorging a little on the depressing side. In fact, the two of us were barely picking at the gooey mess on the table, our conversation limited to an occasional grunt of one syllable, when Ron suddenly straightened up in the booth and pushed his paper plate away.

"I don't know why I'm letting it bum me out like this," he said. "Of course your aunt's right."

I grunted encouragingly so he'd go on.

"The police will find the connection just like I said they would when we were arguing in Susan Kilgore's apartment, remember?"

"But not through the safety deposit box key," I mentioned offhandedly.

"Why not?" he asked, narrowing his eyes. "Lisa, why not the key?"

I reached into my shoulder bag and showed him why not.

"How! . . . Why? . . ."

It was almost a shame to tell him. I was getting to like the way he looked with his mouth wide open in astonishment.

"Ze hand, Monsieur," I said, making the motion of taking a painting off a wall, "ees quicker zen ze eye. Or, anyway, the rubber glove is."

"Why?"

"I honestly don't know the answer to that." I shrugged. "Instinct, I guess."

"You realize, of course, that I should make you take that back up to your aunt right now."

"Sure. But then my aunt would just have it sent anonymously to the police together with the letter which I also palmed and you and I wouldn't have any reason to take another ride out to Mr. Foster Llewelyn's little shack in the hills."

"Now what reason do we have?" he asked skeptically.

"I was just figuring that Miss Williams was probably in a very emotional state when she wrote that letter, and maybe she made a mistake when she wrote that postscript about 'Niobe heeding the call of her father.' Maybe she meant to write 'heeding the call of *your* father'?"

"Who would be Foster Llewelyn."

"Right. And that 'heeding the call' bit does sound like she's going to somebody who needs help."

"And Foster Llewelyn did seem like a very sick man."

"Maybe it's not very much to go on, Ron, but it's better than sitting around here pretending that we're enjoying this pizza."

Ron was already sliding out of the booth. "Miss Williams deserves our best shot," he said. "No matter how slim it might seem."

This time we were admitted to the house. It didn't even take much persuading of the Eskimo. Which I thought was strange until we were escorted to the room where Foster Llewelyn was lying propped up in a makeshift bed and staring out the high, arched window at his domain.

He didn't even turn his head when we entered the room. He just muttered, "Thank you, Man."

He seemed as though he didn't mind our presence, and in trying to figure out why, it occurred to me that he was a man who had done very little talking in his life and was trying to make up for it.

"I call him 'Man,' you see," he began, gesturing toward the departing servant, his eyes never leaving the window, "because his people are called 'The Men'! That's the name of his tribe in their own lingo. Finest people on earth, the Polar Eskimo. 'Til the white man's civilization gets them. Been with me twenty-six years, 'Man' has. Ever since she left me. You want to know about that, possibly. Thought you'd be back. Hoped it, possibly. Couldn't tell you the first time. Don't like telling things. Like selling them. Didn't think you were fooled. Hard to fool young people today. Hard to fool me. Young or old. Fooled myself with her. Emmaline."

I heard Ron's intake of breath alongside me, but kept my eyes riveted on Mr. Llewelyn. He was going on.

"First time I've said that name to anyone since.

Said it a lot of times inside, possibly." He fell silent, still not looking at us. Finally he said, "Well?"

"Well, what, Mr. Llewelyn?" Ron's voice was husky.

"What about my daughter? You said I had a daughter?"

"Well . . ." Ron hesitated, looked at me, and then said, "She's a model."

"A model what? A model person? A model housewife?"

"I mean she models clothes and things . . . poses for advertisements. Perfumes. Things like that."

"That means she's pretty." The old man stated it as a fact.

"Beautiful," Ron said with conviction.

"She's tall then? Like me." He went on without waiting for an answer. "She make money?"

"Probably around one hundred dollars an hour. Maybe more."

"Pretty damn good," he muttered. "She married? Got any kids?"

"No . . . no kids . . ."

I could tell Ron was getting very uneasy talking about Susan Kilgore as though she were alive. I figured that Mr. Llewelyn had given us the perfect opening so I jumped right in.

"She's divorced. Like you and your wife. Miss . . . Emmaline . . . what about her? Is she here?"

For a second I thought he was going to look at me. But instead he just said, "Dissolved. Not divorced. That's the way they did it up there. 'Cause of the shortage of women, possibly.

"'All right, Foster,' she says, 'so you can ease your conscience I'll accept six thousand dollars. No more and no less and that's the end of it.' Offered her a partnership, told. her straight out that if she hadn't taught me about money I'd still be a two-bit operator somewhere up in the Klondike."

His voice trailed off and I was afraid we were losing him.

"When was that, Mr. Llewelyn? Recently? Did she come here to be your partner?" I tried to get through to him.

"Possibly," he said to someone only he could see and probably in answer to a question only he could hear.

"Mr. Llewelyn, please pay attention. The other day we only thought Miss Williams was in danger. Now we *know*."

For the first time the old man reacted. So did Ron. I could feel his hand on my arm.

"Hard to believe," the old man rasped.

"You'd better believe it," I told him and felt Ron's grip tighten.

"Hard to believe I fathered a girl — not a boy."

"You don't have to worry about it, Mr. Llewelyn — " I couldn't stop myself from shouting. "She's dead!"

I tried to yell something about saving the mother but Ron was literally, physically dragging me from the room. I started to resist but my last glimpse of the old man showed me there was no point. He was still facing directly into the window. Somewhere outside it a single bluejay raised its voice in short, raucous cries. Old Llewelyn had shut his eyes and in the side of his neck a single vein throbbed with the uneven beat of his heart, as if keeping time with the trilling of the circling bird.

17.

There's nothing worse than being accused of having done something bad when you know you haven't. Unless it's being accused of having done something bad when you know you have. Which, unfortunately, was the scene that went down on the ride back to town. It was a real bummer. Twenty miles of non-stop blame.

"I should have known better than to listen to you and your ridiculous schemes."

That was for openers. But dear Ron had a lot more where that came from.

"That was terrible, telling him his daughter was dead. That sick old man had nothing to tell us. You just tormented him."

I knew I was in the wrong, so of course I couldn't admit it. I hate myself when I'm like that, but sometimes I just can't seem to help myself.

"We had to try, didn't we?" I yelled back. "You wouldn't be talking to me like this if we'd found Miss Williams there, would you? How do you think things get accomplished in this world? The trouble with you is that you expect to sit back and let other people do the hard stuff. And then you can make your little wimpy judgements if things don't work out the way you like."

Actually, I probably felt worse about it than he did. I would have given anything to have those words back.

"Well," he said at one point, "I won't make the mistake of trying to 'accomplish' anything with you again."

Then there was silence for a while. And that was even worse, all those horrible things we'd said to each other just left hanging in the air between us. I could see that his hands were gripping the steering wheel so tightly that his knuckles were white.

We were back in town when he said very quietly, "I should have listened to your aunt."

I turned, almost startled at his breaking the silence, but he wouldn't look at me.

"Ron, all I wanted to do was help you find your Miss Williams, that's all." I felt like a dog that had been kicked.

"The only way that you can help is to stay out of it," he said through clenched teeth. "Before you do any more harm. Not that there's much left for you to 'accomplish.' Her daughter's dead, and you've pretty well finished off the father. Even you probably — "

We had stopped for a red light and he was still going on as I opened the door and jumped out.

I ran through the traffic, only half-conscious

of blaring horns and screeching tires. I turned down a side street and kept running and running until every breath I took was like a red-hot knife in my chest. Then I slowed down to a walk. It was starting to get dark out and I just kept walking until I found myself at the next major intersection and I had to stop for the cars barreling past.

I looked up and tried to read the street sign. It was all blurry and that was when I realized that I was crying. I wiped my eyes and saw that it was Santa Monica Boulevard. I turned onto it and started walking as fast as I could again, telling myself that I had to get my head straight. I didn't know what to do. I couldn't go back to my aunt's, that was for sure. She'd probably have the same opinion as Ron. I knew they were probably right, but that only made it worse. I felt alone, abandoned. That made me think of Susan Kilgore being abandoned as a baby and it sent a chill up my spine and I shuddered.

It hadn't been my fault that she'd been killed, it hadn't! But Ron acted as if it was. I never wanted to see him again. Or Aunt Kay either. They'd both turned on me, deserted me. I had this creepy feeling that people were staring at me. Not that there were many people around.

I stopped and looked around. Believe me, I never felt more alone than at that moment. I felt like getting to a phone and calling my mother and begging her to let me come home. "Never," I told myself, "never." They'd like that, the both of them. The three of them, my mother included.

I noticed a little restaurant on the other side

of Santa Monica Boulevard. I could just make out the name: "Ports." I walked across to it and, entering, headed straight for the pay phone. Not to call my mother, either. An idea had begun to form in my mind.

He picked up on the second ring.

"Hello?"

"Hello, Bruce?"

"Who is this?"

"Lisa Farraday."

"Oh. What's up?"

"Well . . . actually, a lot. There have been quite a few developments."

He didn't say anything and of course I knew he was waiting for me to go on. The problem was that having begun I wasn't exactly sure how to proceed.

"I was . . . uh . . . wondering if you could possibly meet me and we could discuss them together?"

"Well, I'm a little tied up just now to tell you the truth, Lisa. Couldn't you give me some idea what it's all about?"

"I . . . we don't like to discuss these matters over the phone."

"Could I speak to your aunt, then?"

"Well, I'm not with Aunt Kay right at this minute."

"I see. Well, why don't I drop by over the weekend sometime and we could go over things then?"

It wasn't going exactly the way I had envisioned it. I was afraid he was going to hang up.

"I found a letter from Miss Williams to her

daughter telling where she's disappeared to."
Which wasn't actually a lie, I told myself. Miss
Williams had said she'd gone to "heed the call
of her father," whatever that meant.

"Then your case is solved, isn't it?"

"Not exactly. It's more complicated than that."

"I still don't understand why you want me?"

That was a good question, all right, but not
one which I was prepared to answer over the
phone. So I just blurted out the first thing that
came into my head.

"And I just left Foster Llewelyn."

There was no response at all to that and I was
afraid I'd made a mistake, that our going to see
the man he was so wary of had only made him
mad and turned him off altogether.

But when his voice finally came, it didn't sound
angry at all. Just interested.

"Is that what you want to discuss?"

"Partly."

"Are you at your aunt's?"

"No. I'm in a restaurant. It's called Ports and
it's on Santa Mon —"

"I know where it is. I'll pick you up on the
corner in twenty minutes. Look for a grey
BMW."

18.

He was right on time. As soon as I'd gotten in and sat alongside him, I asked Bruce if he would mind my playing the radio.

"No," he answered, but without any smile, dazzling or otherwise.

I wasn't just being childish or rude. I had had time to think while I was waiting for him and I'd come up with two good reasons for wanting it on while we drove. First, I wasn't ready yet to answer too many questions and figured a little distraction would be a good idea. The second reason was the main one, as you've probably already figured out.

We headed south, eventually turning out toward the beach.

Unfortunately, the radio didn't hinder him completely.

"I've been wondering about something ever since you called, Lisa." Bruce's opening remark didn't come until we'd swung off Sepulveda and up across Sunset Boulevard. "Why me? Why, all

147

of a sudden, am I being included in what's happening?"

I looked out the window while I collected my thoughts and noticed a sign saying Pacific Palisades. So we were definitely heading toward the ocean. I wondered why and thought that asking would give me more time to think of an answer to his question.

"Where are we going?"

"Well, I cancelled a dinner date to meet you and I thought you might be as hungry as I am."

"Starved."

"If you like seafood, there's a quiet little place off the coast highway that does some really tasty shrimps in wine sauce."

"That sounds great," I said and meant it. "Thank you."

"Good. It'll be a perfect place to talk, too."

He spun the wheel expertly and the BMW responded with the smooth power of a race horse, darting across the lanes and up the entrance ramp of the freeway.

"Speaking of talking," he said when we were gliding down the road at a steady fifty-five miles an hour, "you haven't answered my question, you know."

"Well, you did say the other night that you'd give a lot to know how much we knew. I just thought that if I told you, you might be able to really help a lot more."

"I was under the impression that I had been helping a lot. But, all right, what I want to know is what went on between you and Foster Llewelyn. You said you've seen him and I want to know what that aunt of yours told him?"

"Aunt Kay wasn't even there."

"You mean she just sent you?" He shook his head. "You're putting me on. A kid . . . to that old pirate? C'mon, now!" He laughed.

"I was very discreet, Bruce, I assure you." It certainly was flattering to see how much faith everybody had in me.

"I might as well know the worst," he groaned. "Tell me about it."

I felt like I had jumped from the frying pan into the fire. He was being almost as rotten as Ron. To tell you the truth I don't really know if I would have been able to deal with it if I hadn't gotten the first break of that entire miserable day just then.

It was the news coming over the radio. You've probably figured out already that that was the most important reason I wanted it on. Obviously Aunt Kay hadn't lost any time in having Mrs. Di notify the police, just as she said she would.

The newscaster was brief and horribly to the point:

"A bulletin just in. The body of a young woman, identified as Susan Kilgore, a fashion and TV model, age twenty-five, was found earlier today in her Los Angeles apartment. Authorities believe death resulted from massive cerebral injuries and have definitely established it as a homicide. First reports have tentatively ruled out robbery as a motive. The police investigated as the result of an anonymous phone call and are seeking the dead woman's former husband for questioning."

I looked over at Bruce.

"Well?" he asked, "you going to tell me or not?"

"Didn't you hear that?"

"What?"

"On the radio just now?"

"About a murder or something?"

"That's a part of what I have to tell you."

"What are you talking about? What does some model's murder have to do with your missing teacher?" He looked at me as if I was making it up.

We were pulling into the parking lot of a restaurant. I knew I had a lot of convincing ahead of me if I was going to get his cooperation.

"Let's sit down first, Bruce. It's going to take me a while."

I will say this for Bruce Downley. He may have been the walking computer with a kind of single-minded devotion to success that Mr. Gulden said he was, but he also had style. The restaurant was lovely. Very dark and intimate, almost romantic.

Since we were both hungry we ordered immediately. Bruce requested a wine list and asked me if I thought my aunt would object to my having a small glass.

"I think that would be all right," I told him.

"Well, a lot of young people today go overboard with alcohol but you strike me as being more together than that. And, to tell you the truth, you look like you could stand a little something."

"For sure," I admitted. "Today has been the pits."

"Well, you've certainly aroused my curiosity. I hope you're finally ready to satisfy it?"

The wine had come and I have to confess that it wasn't the only thing responsible for the glow I began to experience. When he really tried to communicate with you, Bruce Downley projected an incredible warmth.

"Maybe for openers," he said, "you could begin by telling me how you already knew about a murder that just came over the news."

"Well, Aunt Kay had been notified by a friend of hers, from the District Attorney's office I think it was, as soon as the body was found. But we had to keep it in confidence until it was made public. That's why I had the radio on." A tiny fib. I had to respect Aunt Kay's wish to keep our involvement to a minimum. "They also had a letter Susan wrote incriminating her exhusband."

"But why would they notify your aunt about a murder?"

"Because Susan Kilgore, the murdered woman, was the daughter of Miss Williams, and since Aunt Kay had already contacted them for help in finding the missing mother, they knew of her interest."

"I see." He didn't sound convinced. "Didn't you say something over the phone about having a letter to this daughter? How did you come by that?"

"Aunt Kay got the daughter to come to see her," I explained. Putting it that way it wasn't a direct lie, just a little misleading. I am basically a truthful person, maybe too truthful, and I found that being Aunt Kay's confidential assistant and field investigator was a tricky business. Which made me remember, with a pang, that my status was definitely in doubt after the events of the day.

Bruce looked up, saw the waiter approaching with a loaded tray, and waited until after he'd left.

"Lisa," he said, "I think it would be better if you just told me what's on your mind instead of my constantly interrupting your train of thought with questions." Then he smiled for the first time. "But I still reserve the right to ask questions afterward. Is it a deal?"

"It's a deal," I said, forked my first bite of seafood crepe, and began. Naturally I skipped the part about going to Susan Kilgore's apartment and finding her there, dead. But I covered both visits to Foster Llewelyn thoroughly, except, of course, my telling him that his daughter was dead. I still felt so guilty about that, I wouldn't have been able to bring myself to mention it anyway. And, even though at first I hadn't thought I would, I wound up telling Bruce about my fight with Ron too. I guess that was bothering me so much I had to talk about it. Bruce was very sympathetic and accepted the version I gave him. He seemed to know all about Mister Llewelyn's failing health and never questioned

152

Ron's getting angry at me for harassing somebody that ill.

When I'd finished, Bruce gave a little low whistle of astonishment. "That's really an incredible piece of detective work that you've come up with, Lisa. It seems to me that you've just about got it nailed down that Foster Llewelyn was once married to your missing teacher and actually could have fathered her daughter."

"There doesn't seem to be any doubt about it," I declared proudly.

"You say that old Llewelyn was suspicious that one of his business rivals put you up to questioning him?"

"Maybe at first," I admitted. "He even mentioned Mr. Gulden and those other two names."

"Perkins and McVay. I know of them." He was thoughtful for a moment. "Did he say he was going to make an investigation at the bank? You know I've warned you that my position in this is very delicate."

"Bruce, I didn't mention you. And neither did Mr. Llewelyn."

"He wouldn't even know my name. Stars don't notice spear-carriers."

"Honestly, I don't think he cared. I don't think he cares about anything anymore," I added guiltily, thinking that I probably had helped him not to care anymore.

"I believe you."

He smiled and took my hand. "You're an amazing girl — young woman," he corrected himself. "How old are you, anyway?"

"I'll be seventeen in September."

"You've got brains. And determination. I doubt if you are fully aware of what a remarkable combination that is."

He looked down and seemed to be aware for the first time that he was holding my hand. He released it, patted it, and smiled a sad, half-smile. "It doesn't necessarily bring happiness, being different, Lisa. Other people tend not to understand."

"Really," I said. "Tell me about it."

He laughed. "That's right, you know all about it now, don't you? You've already encountered that attitude with your boyfriend."

"Ron isn't exactly my boyfriend," I heard myself saying. "In that area he hardly knows I'm alive." It was amazing the things I felt comfortable telling that man, even though he was much older than me.

"But you want him to be, is that it?"

I felt myself flush and Bruce said kindly, "You don't have to answer that. I'm afraid I've strayed into a very personal area. Let's get back to business, shall we? You said before that Mr. Llewelyn gave credit to your friend's teacher, Miss Williams, for his financial success? Do you suppose that she might be involved in that area now with him? I mean she wouldn't have to be physically at his house to be engaged in some of his operations, checking his holdings, that sort of thing?"

"There wasn't any indication of that, no. But maybe we should talk about it." I felt myself getting excited again. "Bruce, you know, from the first moment that I thought of calling you I knew that if we put our heads together, we'd come up with the clue to her whereabouts."

"Correct me if I'm wrong, Lisa" — there was a half-smile playing on his lips — "but didn't you say that you had a letter which told where she had gone?"

"Well . . ."

"You kind of exaggerated, is that it?"

I nodded. "I hope you're not angry."

"I'm sincerely flattered. You must have really wanted my help."

Bruce motioned to the waiter who came over and cleared the table.

"How does a café espresso with a twist of lemon sound to you?"

"It sounds fabulous." While he was ordering I made up my mind. There was no holding back anymore. I reached into my bag, brought out the "Niobe" letter, and unfolded it and spread it out on the table so Bruce and I could go over it together.

19.

Bruce studied the letter while I sipped café espresso which, if you haven't ever had it, sounds a lot better than it is. Bruce broke his concentration only once, to have me explain the significance of the name "Niobe." Finally he looked up.

"Lisa, if you can see any clue in this letter then you're a lot more perceptive than I am."

I guess my face must have fallen because he immediately leaned forward and stretched his hand out to squeeze my shoulder reassuringly.

"I know how let-down you must feel. You've done everything you possibly could. But you can't work miracles, Lisa. You can't find something that isn't there."

"Then you don't think that postscript about 'heeding the call of her father' means anything?"

"Not to me it doesn't."

"I guess taking this letter was just another example of my 'appalling conduct' and 'betrayal of trust.' I can't seem to do anything right. I should have left it for my aunt to turn over to the police. It might be a clue to finding the murderer if it can't help us find Miss Williams."

"You're too quick to blame yourself, Lisa. This letter and your teacher's disappearance don't have anything to do with the murder. But, I'll tell you what I'll do, if you'd like. I have friends who have a laboratory. They could run some tests on it. Fingerprints, chemical analysis of the paper and ink, and so on, any traces of anything at all. It's a long shot but maybe they could turn something up and that way it wouldn't be official. You wouldn't have the police harassing you or your aunt. If you'd feel comfortable entrusting it to me?"

"Bruce, no matter how this turns out, I'm glad I called you. They were beginning to make me feel like a complete air-head."

"I'm sure your aunt has a higher opinion of you than that. Together you make a good team. I imagine if the two of you put your heads together on her theory that the ex-husband murdered that poor girl, you might really come up with something."

"Well, it's true that Aunt Kay doesn't seem to think the letter and the murder are connected. I mean, she seems pretty sure it's the ex-husband."

"From what you've told me, and that's all I have to go on, everything points in his direction."

"It's just so hard to imagine someone whom you were in love with and who loved you killing you, that's all."

"I'm afraid, as you get older, Lisa, you'll learn something about the darker side of people's passions. Remember, the radio did say the police were looking for him."

"I think that's the most horrible thing in the world. Love turning to hate." And a part deep inside me was thinking how close I had come to hating Ron.

"Life does strange things to people. We're in no position to judge him. A guy who's been in Vietnam. It's hard for us to even imagine what somebody goes through in that situation."

"I guess you're right. Would you excuse me please," I said, folding up the letter and dropping it back in my bag. "I have to go to the Ladies Room."

If you're thinking that my leaving the table was done abruptly, you should have seen my action when I got to the back of the restaurant. As I feared, there was no exit, but there was a door which, judging from the noise behind it, obviously led to the kitchen. I didn't hesitate; I just hustled myself right on through and past stoves and sinks and waiting hot platters, ignoring the startled cries of outraged cooks. There was a screen door at the far end, and I pushed through and found myself outside in the parking lot.

At the extreme corner of the lot I could make out a grove of trees and underbrush that seemed to extend along the highway. I edged my way around the rows of parked cars and headed for it.

In case you think I'd lost my mind, far from it. I knew I had to find some heavy cover. Once amongst the trees and shrubbery, I planned on following the shoulder of the road back to the small shopping center which I remembered passing on the way in, and which I hoped had a public phone.

You see, the shopping center wasn't the only thing I had remembered. I'd also remembered that the bulletin on the radio hadn't said anything about Susan Kilgore's ex-husband being a Vietnam veteran. Ron had gotten that information from New York in tracking down Susan Kilgore herself. And, since I knew I sure as heck hadn't mentioned it, how did Bruce Downley know? Also, I had enough common sense to wonder what good having that letter chemically analyzed would do. Unless it was just a good excuse for getting it away from me?

Don't think I didn't have some doubts about what I was doing. But if it was another of my mistakes, I'd apologize later. Only, some instinct told me not to let him have that letter. And, if I was right, I couldn't risk making him suspicious by refusing. Not while I was within grabbing distance. I'd not forgotten how Susan Kilgore looked lying there on the floor of her bedroom. For that same reason I hadn't wanted to take a chance on phoning from the restaurant.

I never heard him. I was in the darkest part of the lot, almost to the trees, when his arm hooked me around the neck so tightly I couldn't scream. And then his smooth, soft voice purred in my ear.

"You should have left the letter, cookie. I might not have realized in time if you hadn't snatched it up so suddenly."

Even if I'd had an answer to that I couldn't have gotten it out. Not with the choke hold he was using to drag me across the lot to his car.

"You turned into another unpleasant surprise. Just like those checks made out to an Emmaline Williams when I first came across them among old Llewelyn's books. Just like you, I figured out what they might signify. Of course, I had the advantage of knowing a lot more about him. In fact, I *am* him, you might say. At least as far as his holding companies, bearer bonds, and most of his negotiable assets are concerned."

He was grunting and straining with the effort, but I also remembered with a horrible irony how the first thing I'd noticed about him was what great physical shape he was in.

"Then you two brats breezed into my office with buttermouth Bertram, playing coy little games with me about finding the one person I was worried about."

He'd gotten the car door open and as the little light flickered on I could see his face by it, his mouth twisted with the strain into a terrifying mockery of that dazzling smile.

"That was my biggest mistake, scaring the old lady off before she led me to the daughter. Luckily, you and that old blind biddy who thinks she's the Duchess of Pasadena handed her to me on a silver platter."

He'd dragged most of me into the car and was folding my legs under me so I'd fit across his front seat.

"She was a tough monkey, that daughter. She had some of old Llewelyn in her, all right. But

160

that also made it easy. The greedy ones are always easy."

He was kneeling on me, sliding over to get behind the wheel. As soon as I felt his arm loosen, I opened my mouth to scream. And he gagged it with his handkerchief.

"That's a good girl," he said, tying my hands behind me. "I hope you aren't *too* good a girl, Lisa. It'll look better if you have a history of being wild. Not that it matters, really; the police are always ready to believe the worse about you kids today, with drugs and all."

He fumbled in the glove compartment and brought out what looked like one of those little plastic nasal sprays.

"You look frightened, Lisa," he murmured, peering into my eycs. "I hate to see that. Sooner or later people always get frightened of me. It's because they know somewhere at the core of their beings that I'm capable of doing the things they only dare fantasize about."

He stuck the spray bottle into my mouth but I bit down with all my might and clamped it shut.

"Don't fight it, Lisa," he said, applying pressure. "Make it easy on yourself. Sooner or later I'll get enough of it into you, and if you fight you might choke because of the gag and choking's a horrible way to die. The thorazine will make you groggy so I can take off the gag and untie your hands. The LSD is just for the Medical Examiner so there'll be an explanation of why you drove my car off the sea wall into the oc — "

I just barely had time to react to the crash.

161

I'd seen the headlights coming up fast behind Bruce Downley's shoulder. The impact sprung the driver's side door, where my head was, open and knocked me sprawling halfway out. I swung my legs up and backward-somersaulted the rest of the way, landing in the gravel parking lot in time to see the out of control car ram the BMW again.

For one scary split-second I saw Bruce Downley looking around for me, but there was that crazy car coming straight for him again and, instead of bothering with me, he started his engine and roared out of the parking lot with both doors swinging open wildly.

The other car spun around after him and for a second I was blinded in the glare of its headlights as their beams swept across me. Not wanting to be just an ordinary hit-and-run accident after having just missed being a homicide, I rolled away and over and over as fast as I could.

Until I was hooked by a strong arm. Only this time, instead of being hurt by Bruce Downley, I was being hugged. By Ron.

"Are you all right, Lisa? Answer me, you crazy fool! What happened? Are you all right? Can't you —"

But I'm not going to relate it exactly, because you know the way people say things under stress like that. They just keep saying the same things over and over. Which sounded beautiful to me at the time, but makes awfully dumb reading later.

Of course when he finally pulled the gag out, I had some brilliant things to say myself, like:

"Oh, Ron! Ron. Ronnie. Where? How? Ron, oh, Ron . . ."

But since he was still holding me close to untie my hands and pressing me all over (no doubt to make sure there were no broken bones) I, at least, had the presence of mind to show him a better use for mouths than asking questions or serving as a hamper for soiled handkerchiefs. He seemed to appreciate it even more than shaking hands goodnight.

"Oh, Lisa, I was afraid I'd waited too long."

"You sure did," I agreed, meeting his lips with mine again, "but you're making up for lost time now."

"I meant getting you away from Downley," he said, trying to look stern.

"Of course. Did you think I meant something else?"

He decided to take that opportunity to look around at the people gawking out of the restaurant at us.

"I'd better call your aunt," he said and led me tenderly through the assortment of waiters, kitchen help, and customers who had congregated in the entrance. I had to lean on him, having started trembling and shaking all over as the excitement wore off and the realization set in. I had come very close to tying the world record for deep diving without an aqualung, a record nobody ever breaks. I could feel the shards of broken glass from the cars crunching under my feet as we walked.

The hostess from the restaurant came out and escorted me inside the Ladies Room while Ron went to phone. "You all right, honey? What was it? A couple of jealous boyfriends?" She was a middle-aged lady with a very motherly quality.

"You could say that." I wasn't up for explanations.

"And the woman is always the one in the middle, right?" She nodded sympathetically. "You're lucky. You could really have gotten yourself hurt."

Just before I got inside the Ladies Room I heard somebody say, "That's the kid that guy was looking for. The one he said flipped out on drugs."

So Bruce Downley had already laid the groundwork for my "accident."

No wonder they believed him, I thought to myself when I saw my reflection in the Ladies Room mirror. I was a wreck. My hair all over the place, clothes torn, and bits of gravel from the parking lot still stuck to me. My lips were puffed and bruised from the spray bottle, I could hardly move my neck, and my entire body felt like somebody had been using it for a trampoline.

When I came out after putting myself together as best I could, the hostess told me Ron was outside.

"You sure you don't want me to call a doctor, honey?"

"Thanks, but it's not that bad. I'll be all right once I get home."

"I know it's not my place to say, but the one who took off? That guy's too old for you, honey."

I didn't say anything to that, just thanked her for her concern again. But I did think to myself

164

that if I had my way, Bruce Downley wouldn't get any older.

Outside, Ron was kneeling alongside his car examining the wrinkled fender and smashed headlight. The engine was running.

"In case I haven't thanked you, thank you. As they say in the movies, you saved my life."

"Anytime," he said offhandedly but gave my neck a short squeeze which I didn't mind despite the pain. He patted the old Maverick. "Well, it doesn't look so hot, but it'll get us back all right. Needless to say, your aunt is waiting expectantly."

"I'll bet."

"What're you looking for?"

"You won't believe this — a nasal spray. But it must have fallen down inside Downley's car."

"Maybe you'd like to tell me just exactly what was going on?"

"On the ride home," I said, crawling in and collapsing. "On the ride home."

20.

It took me almost the entire ride to tell it all. That was partly Ron's fault. He kept interrupting with pointed little comments on how naive I was. Also, it was hard for me to keep my mind on my story when I was dying to hear *his*. He insisted, though, that he'd tell how he found me later. And there was no denying that he had earned the right to choose.

As I reached the point where he'd rescued me and found myself starting to thank him again, Ron cut me short.

"But I still can't believe you were that gullible. It was such an obvious snow job; that's what gets me. You just lapped up all those compliments and never realized the mind games he was laying on you."

"It's easy to say that now that Bruce Downley has revealed himself," I reminded him, "but don't forget that even my aunt trusted him enough to ask him to keep helping us."

"Don't *you* forget," he said smugly, "I never trusted him. Not from the first time we saw him."

That was my opening and I jumped on it.

"You were just jealous. That's all that was."

"You're out of your head. Jealous of what?"

"Now really, Ron." I was relishing the opportunity. "How *did* you just happen to be in the parking lot of that restaurant?"

"I followed you there," he answered promptly.

I pounced. "You couldn't have followed me; I would have noticed. You had to be following him when he picked me up. Now what made you do that? It couldn't have been that after the fight we had you were worried I'd go to Bruce Downley, could it, Ron?" I didn't need to be a computer genius to have figured that out.

"You know you provided him with a perfect cover story when you told him about our fight." Ron had neatly changed the subject. "He told those people in the restaurant that you were extremely depressed and talking about suicide because of a fight with your boyfriend. Then he made a big show of "discovering" that some thorazine his doctor had prescribed for him was missing. He was setting up your 'accident-suicide' very nicely."

"That doesn't make me feel any better about letting him get away scot-free like that."

"Your aunt said to come straight back. You can bet she's doing something about him."

Ron found a parking space close to the hotel and, getting out of the car, I noticed his gaze stray sadly over the damaged fender and headlight.

"Aunt Kay'll take it off your bill, I'm sure."

"The insurance will cover most of it I guess," he said, offering me his arm to lean on. Actually I was feeling almost myself again but I took it anyway. There's no point in making an obsession of being strong and resourceful.

Aunt Kay was at her desk in the study, talking on the phone.

"Yes," she was saying, "that all fits. No, I'm afraid his sense of self-preservation will alert him to the necessity of absconding immediately with what he has. I hope it's not futile, but I plan to add a murder charge to that. My client has just walked in and I must speak to him and my grand-niece. I appreciate your extraordinary efforts to-night and I will call you if something I have in mind develops."

She hung up and assumed an expectant air. I'd have loved to ask how she could tell it was us, but I knew she wouldn't answer, and there was something else I wanted to know a lot worse.

"Was that the police, Aunt Kay? Haven't they arrested him yet?"

"What would they arrest him for? Trying to prevent his distraught dinner companion from taking drugs?"

"How did you know th — ?"

"Mr. Van Cleave had ascertained that much when he called me. It would be a matter of your word against his. Besides, Mr. Downley has laid his plans carefully and well in advance, including, I am sure, a secure and instant escape route across the border to Mexico, so they would not find him, anyway. Not without a full-scale manhunt with extradition orders. And to galvanize the authorities to undertake an action of that magnitude we need more than suspicion, conjecture, and the unsupported testimony of a teen-age girl. Confound it, we need your Miss Williams, Mr. Van Cleave. I'm not wrong about that last part, am I, Lisa? He did reveal himself to you?"

"It was like he was compelled to, Aunt Kay," I told her, and then gave her a brief account of the things which had made me suspicious and the stuff he'd said while dragging me along the parking lot. When I was done, Aunt Kay's expression had turned very thoughtful.

"Now, Lisa," she began slowly, "you no doubt anticipate severe chastisement for your escapade today, and justifiably. But if you cannot learn from what you went through tonight, then you are truly beyond redemption. There is another factor which inclines me toward leniency. That you were right about Miss Williams' letter. The postscript did contain the clue to Miss Williams' destination."

"What is it?" I was already pulling the letter out of my bag.

"That's your third question, Lisa. Bear with me while I go back and answer the first one. Just before you arrived, Mr. Gulden called from his office at the First Industrial Bank & Trust Co."

"From his office?" Ron asked it before I could. "At this hour?"

"I called him just after I dispatched you to watch Mr. Bruce Downley's house."

"Aunt Kay, you *sent* Ron to watch Bruce

Downley?" I looked from her to Ron. He made a little smiling, shrugging gesture as if to say, "sorry to disillusion you about being jealous."

"Yes, dear," Aunt Kay was going on, "it seemed a wise precaution after Mr. Van Cleave told me of your argument and subsequent departure in traffic. You see, I had begun to have second thoughts. You may recall my asking if you were both positive that the letter you saw in Ms. Kilgore's typewriter made no mention of either the money which had fallen into her hands or the mother who had put it there?"

We both said, "Yes," and Ron added, "I asked you, just before we went for pizza, if that meant something and you said, 'probably not.' "

Aunt Kay nodded. "It was only a glimmer, then. But my mental processes were stimulated. If the letter wasn't about that, what was it about? You said it dwelt mostly on Ms. Kilgore's stormy relationship with her ex-husband. It struck me that was not only suspiciously convenient, but also not in character. The natural way for her to communicate those sort of spicy tidbits would be over the telephone, where she could have the instant gratification of her listener's reaction and response. It was also suggestive that this letter which placed her violent ex-husband at the murder scene was typed and therefore couldn't be checked with Ms. Kilgore's handwriting. In fact, it couldn't be checked with anything. Never divulging a specific name, place, date, or fact, except for the references to her work and her ex-husband, it could have been written about

170

anybody, *by* anybody. But who could implicate her husband? And who would benefit from her death? Of course the answer to that could be any number of people about whom we know nothing. But the fact remained that Susan Kilgore had been killed at the height of our investigation of her mother's disappearance, an investigation in which she figured prominently, and she had been here to see us. I decided to proceed on the assumption that the murder and the disappearance of Miss Williams were linked."

"After putting me down for acting like they were," I said bitterly.

"It was only an assumption. To establish some grounds for it, I phoned the bank and caught Mr. Gulden before he left for the day. I posed a hypothesis: based on modern computer techniques, would it be possible, theoretically, for someone with knowledge and access to embezzle and to hide any record of his actions through deft programming of the computers? Mr. Gulden was skeptical at first, but he could not, he admitted finally, give me an irrevocable 'no.' 'In this technological world we live in, anything is possible,' were his closing words. I had accomplished two things: I had tested my hypothesis and I had planted a seed in his mind."

"You mean you suspected Downley already?" Ron sounded pretty skeptical himself.

" 'Suspected' is too strong a word. Nevertheless, my basic hypothesis rested on it being someone who had knowledge of certain facts in the case. I even considered Bert Gulden himself, but dismissed him as being too honest and too un-imaginative. Besides, why would he have helped us?"

"But the same applies to Downley. Why did *he*?" The skepticism hadn't left Ron's voice. "That's something I've been wondering about."

"But the same conditions didn't apply. Bert Gulden could have told us, in a nice way, to simply go to the devil. Mr. Downley knew that a refusal would have risked arousing Mr. Gulden's curiosity, not to mention his hostility. And, remember, it was a chore which could have been done by a clerk at Mr. Gulden's direction. No, Downley couldn't risk anyone else making those inquiries. He had to take the risk of feeding us bits of 'helpful' information. Naturally he also had to find out what we knew, and that led to his coming here and staging a dramatic scene to convince us that he was fearful of compromising his position by helping us. In a way, of course, he really was. The real emotion showing through was what made it effective."

"You tell him, Aunt Kay," I said, looking at Ron. "Bruce Downley was awfully convincing, wasn't he?"

"More than that, by the time Mr. Van Cleave called to ask if you had come here after abruptly departing his company, I was in a quandry. We were still no closer to finding Miss Williams. Nor could I get around the fact that if my theory was correct, the killer knew who Susan Kilgore was, knew her connection with Miss Williams, knew where she lived, knew she was a model, and knew her husband had served in Vietnam. But how could Mr. Downley have that knowledge?"

She stopped and poured herself a glass of water from her pitcher.

"It was hearing your voice on the phone, telling me that Lisa was missing, Mr. Van Cleave. It recalled to my mind that bit of dialogue between you and she on the night that Mr. Downley was here. Do you remember? It was after he left and just before you went home yourself?"

I was racking my brain. I glanced over at Ron and saw he was doing the same. How could Ron's telling her I was missing make my aunt remember? Missing! I got it!

"That piece of paper. Ron wrote the information from New York about Susan Kilgore on a piece of paper I gave him, and later it wasn't where Ron said he'd left it. And I put Bruce Downley in this room while we ate dinner. Alone. In here with that piece of paper. Oh, Aunt Kay—" My lower lip was trembling so I could hardly say it. "He told me we gave him the d-daughter on a silver pl- pl-" I couldn't hold back. Sobs were racking my whole body.

"It's like I k-killed her."

Then there was a strong arm around me for the second time that night, comforting me.

"Not alone." Ron's voice was husky. "Not without plenty of help. I'm the one who left the paper."

"Rubbish." Aunt Kay was harsh. "If guilt is to be apportioned, we are all three equally indictable. But for what crime? There was no way we could know then. The important thing is that we know now. Sitting here wallowing in self-recrimination will not bring Susan Kilgore's killer to justice. It will not find her mother."

She held out the box of tissues from her desk and Ron took some and gave them to me.

"The seed I planted in Mr. Gulden's mind has already begun to bear fruit." Aunt Kay was all business. Seeing the expression on her face I could almost pity Bruce Downley.

"Mr. Gulden decided to stay behind after the bank closed and do some checking himself. That call I received just before you came in was to inform me that he had uncovered evidence of a remarkably inventive swindle.

"It was the declining health and character of Mr. Llewelyn himself which provided the opportunity for Mr. Downley's insidious skills. A lone wolf, with no close associates, friends, or family, there was no one to safeguard his interests as his faculties of mind and body deteriorated.

"In the short time he has had so far, Mr. Gulden has been able to uncover illegal transfer of assets, hidden holding corporations, stock manipulation, false letters of credit, and the first steps toward gaining control of various foreign and domestic accounts through 'creative' computer programming. Also of interest is that these activities apparently speeded up about the time Miss Williams disappeared. That seems to corroborate what Downley blurted out to you, Lisa, that he deduced from that old check to Emmaline Williams the one possibly fatal flaw: an heir. Threatened with the destruction of his plans, he struck ruthlessly, and killed Susan Kilgore.

"And that brings us full circle to where we began — the missing teacher, her mother, Emmaline Williams."

"And the clue, Aunt Kay?" I blew my nose in the last tissue and Ron sat back down in his chair.

"You said that you found the clue to where she is in that postscript?" he reminded her.

"It was actually obvious, if I'd only been alert enough to see it," she replied. "Miss Williams told us straight out. She said 'heed the call of *Niobe*'s father,' not *her* father and certainly not Mr. Llewelyn, her daughter's father. Mrs. Di-Pasquale looked up Niobe's father for me in my Oxford Classical Dictionary. He turned out to be Tantalus, who, because he could not be killed, was sentenced to eternal punishment, with everything he wanted always just out of reach. It's from his name that we get our word, tantalize."

She settled back in her chair with a look of satisfaction.

"I don't see the connection, Aunt Kay."

"Eternal punishment, life imprisonment in modern terms. Now there are new programs of education and re-adjustment aimed at those unfortunate people who, like Tantalus, are not killed, but face lifelong punishment or the tantalizing possibility of parole. Needless to say, teachers are desperately needed for those programs. At least that was what my friend, Mr. Phillips, at the Attorney General's office told me when I called him."

"You mean you think Miss Williams is teaching at a prison?" Ron's tone wasn't skeptical exactly. More like wanting to believe.

"Not 'think,' Mr. Van Cleave. I *know*. Mr. Phillips made the arrangements and I shall be talking to Miss Williams by telephone in the morning."

Ron and I exchanged open-mouthed looks and then we were both on our feet, rushing to Aunt Kay's desk.

"Aunt Kay!" I wanted to hug her.

"Mrs. Farraday . . . ," Ron was saying, " . . . that's . . . that's . . . will I be able to see her?"

"You've done it, Aunt Kay!" At last, I was saying inside, at last.

"Done what?" Aunt Kay snapped it out.

"Nearly gotten my only grandniece murdered? Yes, I've done that. And while she was entrusted to my care! Served coffee and brandy to the swindler and murderer who tried to kill her? That's what I've done."

"But you'll get him now, Aunt Kay. With Mr. Gulden's evidence —"

"We have nothing that I, myself, couldn't tear to shreds if I were Bruce Downley's defense counsel. He'll never be brought to justice unless Miss Williams comes forth with her story. You asked about seeing her, Mr. Van Cleave? I fervently hope so. I expect your presence and concern to weigh heavily with her. Right now the best thing you can do is leave me in peace. Get some rest. You too, Lisa.

"I am a tired old woman who must think of some way to compel another tired old woman to travel the nearly one hundred miles from the state prison at Tehachapi to face the life she has run from. The only life she ever created. And now I must ask her to face its death and the death of her dream. Go. Leave me to deal with that and with myself."

We left her.

21.

However Aunt Kay dealt with those things, she dealt with them successfully enough to bring Miss Williams. Mrs. Di woke me from a nightmarish-tossed sleep to inform me that as soon as I was washed and dressed I was to call Ron and tell him to hurry over.

When the doorbell sounded, he and I were having a cup of coffee in the kitchen with Mrs. Di. She said she'd get it, so we took our cups into the study to wait with Aunt Kay.

The way Ron had described Miss Williams, especially her old-fashioned virtues and utter disregard for fashion and all, I guess I expected to see someone dressed appropriately for sitting in a convertible and watching a parade of soldiers returning home from the Second World War. But the straight-backed, elderly woman Mrs. Di brought into the study had on a smartly tailored suit and sensible, but not completely unstylish, gray shoes. She was tall and the nose above the determined mouth and strong chin was long and pointed. The main feature was her eyes. They were black and piercing.

She advanced two steps into the room, saw Ron as he stood up from his chair, and said, "Oh," without realizing she'd said it.

"You know Mr. Van Cleave," Aunt Kay said. "And this is my grandniece, Lisa Farraday."

She acknowledged me with a nod of her head but her eyes never left Ron.

"Are you responsible for this, Ronald?" Her voice was a surprise, very pleasant and mellow.

"Mr. Van Cleave was only concerned for your safety, Miss Williams. Won't you please be seated?"

She sat and transferred her gaze to Aunt Kay.

"You are blind," she said after a moment.

"Yes. And you are blunt. I'm glad. It allows me to rationalize being equally forthright."

"Somehow I doubt that you need any rationalization," Miss Williams said drily. "Over the phone you threatened to have the Attorney General subpoena me if I did not come to see you."

So that was how "one tired old lady dealt with compelling," etc.

Aunt Kay was going on. "You forced my hand. You refused to even come to the phone until I used the name 'Niobe.'"

"Will you satisfy my curiosity as to how you know the significance of that name to me?"

"My bluntness does not extend to gratuitous cruelty, Miss Williams. I am not sure you are aware of certain events. . . ."

"If you mean the . . . death of a . . . young

woman who might have had a particular letter in her possession ... yes, I am."

She had spoken very slowly, choosing her words. The voice was no longer pleasant and mellow. But it didn't break. .

"I have already told you over the phone that Mr. Van Cleave retained me to find you. Through the extraordinary efforts of my grand-niece, I also found this."

Aunt Kay held up the "Niobe" letter. One glance was enough for Miss Williams.

"At my age," Aunt Kay continued, "time and energy are precious. Please don't waste them by trying to dissuade us from our belief that Susan Kilgore was your daughter."

"I am through . . ." Miss Williams had to pause to clear her throat. ". . . I denied her in life. No more. Yes, Susan Kilgore was my daughter."

"And Foster Llewelyn her father."

"That is of no interest to me and I can't imagine that it would be to you."

"But it is. To explain why, I must first tell you of a death you are not aware of. Approximately two hours ago I received a phone call in accordance with arrangements previously made. The call was to notify me of the death, by natural causes, of Foster Llewelyn."

That was Aunt Kay. She'd had plenty of time to tell us, but of course then it wouldn't have been quite as dramatic.

"Very well, you have told me." Miss Williams was unimpressed.

"Naturally I anticipated no display of grief

after so many years of estrangement. That was merely a preamble to what I am about to tell you."

I watched Miss Williams very closely as Aunt Kay told her, briefly, the story of Bruce Downley's embezzlement of Mr. Llewelyn's fortune. She barely seemed to be listening. When Aunt Kay had finished outlining the scheme for her, she merely asked:

"Is that why you brought me here? Do you think I care if some new breed of freebooter has come along to plunder Foster Llewelyn's ill-gotten gains? He probably stole it in the first place. Legally, of course. He was too crafty to do anything overtly criminal. Even back then he showed a great natural aptitude for the acquisition of wealth."

"And you provided him with the technique, the knowledge."

Miss Williams nodded, the black eyes seeming to get blacker. "I'm a good teacher." She smiled a bitter smile. "A teacher who never learned the one important lesson."

"Yes," Aunt Kay muttered, half under her breath, "a little learning *is* a dangerous thing."

"It was my knowledge that first attracted him to me," Miss Williams said suddenly. "He took an adult course at night that I taught at the local high school. You see, I am older than he is . . . was. Now I really must be going."

"Not before you commit yourself to help bring this man to account for his crimes." There was steel in Aunt Kay's voice.

"I told you, I don't care who has Foster Llewelyn's money. Or how they got it."

"I said *crimes*. Plural, Miss Williams."

The steel had become a whip.

"That same man also killed Susan Kilgore."

"What?" Miss Williams was startled. "Why?"

"He came across that long forgotten original check for six thousand dollars, made out to and cashed by you. And deduced, correctly, that there was an heir who could thwart his scheme."

"I don't believe you!" Miss Williams gathered herself together as if to get up from her chair. "I told you I have to be going."

"Running away this time at the mere mention of him? Last time you ran, at least it was due to his actual physical presence."

"I don't know what you're talking about."

"I think you do. And I think I know Bruce Downley well enough to know that he would not write or phone. He called on you in person, inadvertently alarmed you, and that is why you fled."

"You have a very active imagination."

"Lisa," Aunt Kay snapped. "Describe for Miss Williams the man who called on her."

There she was again. Suppose I blew it because she hadn't prepared me? But, of course, if she had, it wouldn't have been nearly as dramatic as just springing it out of the blue that way.

I turned to Miss Williams and, conscious of Ron's eyes burning two holes in my back, gave her a total description of Bruce Downley, right down to the dazzling smile and purring voice.

At first she met my eyes defiantly, but by the time I was through and she spoke, her eyes were on the carpet at her feet.

"He had identification saying he was an investigator for the Internal Revenue Service. But I'm not unacquainted with IRS methods, and some of his questions didn't ring true. After he'd gone, I decided . . . well, obviously you know what I decided." She looked up at Aunt Kay. "You know a great deal."

"But the authorities do not. They do not know there is an eyewitness who can identify Mr. Downley and place him at the door of Susan Kilgore's real mother. They do not even know there is a real mother."

Aunt Kay reached for the pitcher, thought better of it, and brought the hand back to her desk top before continuing.

"The lady who admitted you, Mrs. DiPasquale, is a Notary Public. Without a signed, notarized statement from you, any case against that man will be unsupported by motive. The police will not launch the intensive effort necessary to secure his capture and conviction. He is entirely without scruple, Miss Williams. He very nearly murdered the sixteen-year-old girl sitting across from you. Indeed, were it not for the courageous action of your pupil, Mr. Van Cleave, he would have succeeded. The next person who poses a threat to him may not be so fortunate as to have stirred the chivalrous impulses of a quick and resourceful young man."

Ron shot me a look. I raised my eyebrows to show I was innocent.

"Indeed" — Aunt Kay wasn't letting up — "Mr. Downley has already manufactured evidence which may result in an innocent man paying the penalty for his murder of your daughter."

"You're asking me to publicly reveal the one act in my life of which I am ashamed — the abandonment of my only child. What good will it really do? It won't bring her back to life."

"No, your daughter will never know your touch or your voice, your dream of a splendid reconciliation is shattered, but you can still do in death what you failed to do in life — acknowledge your child."

Aunt Kay didn't have to hand the box of tissues to Ron that time. He got up quietly and handed them to Miss Williams, so I guess she was crying. For some reason I couldn't see too well myself.

"Thank you," she mumbled. Then she looked up and said, very clearly, "Thank you for everything, Ronald. When I come back to sign my statement, I'll give you the name of a good tutor to replace me."

Somehow that seemed only right and fitting, that Miss Williams should tell us by way of Ron that she would do it. It had all begun with him, with his caring about what had happened to a good teacher.

Aunt Kay asked, "Miss Williams, you said 'when I come back'? May I suggest that you wait with us? Preparing the statement won't take long."

"No, you may not," Miss Williams replied with dignity. "I'm going now to see my daughter."

"I beg your pardon," Aunt Kay breathed. And then, to herself, "Niobe weeps no more."

I watched Miss Williams stride gracefully from the room, and it struck me that she would never know how much her daughter had resembled her, doing that same thing only a few days, and about a million years, before.

22.

It took them a while, but the police finally found Mr. Bruce Downley in a tiny country called Liechtenstein. It's somewhere between Austria and Switzerland and is one of those places you're always hearing about on TV where they have special tax laws if you're rich and provide anonymous numbered bank accounts. Unfortunately for charming old Bruce, they also have an extradition treaty with the United States and he was brought back to stand trial for the murder of Susan Kilgore.

As I write this, I'm back in Saratoga Springs, a hundred feet of snow has just fallen, and I'm holding a letter I got yesterday from Ron, telling me that he's going to be coming east to spend Christmas with his father.

And, it seems, he just happened to pop up to see Aunt Kay the other day, and when he mentioned his plans, she told him that she and Mrs. Di were planning to be in New York over the holidays and that she was sure she could convince my parents to let me spend my vacation with them. Which would mean, of course, that Ron and I would be together. You can imagine how I feel about that. Not that anything as exciting as what happened last summer could ever possibly occur again.